The SHIP of CLOUD and STARS

ALSO BY AMY RAPHAEL

The Forest of Moon and Sword

A Seat at the Table: Women on the Frontline of Music

A Game of Two Halves: Famous Football Fans Meet Their Heroes

Danny Boyle: Creating Wonder

Mike Leigh on Mike Leigh

The SHIP of CLOUD and STARS

AMY RAPHAEL

Illustrated by
GEORGE ERMOS

Orion

ORION CHILDREN'S BOOKS

First published in Great Britain in 2022 by Hodder & Stoughton

1 3 5 7 9 10 8 6 4 2

A CIP catalogue record for this book
is available from the British Library.

ISBN 978 1 510 10841 7

Typeset in Baskerville by Avon DataSet Ltd,
Arden Court, Alcester, Warwickshire

Printed and bound in Great Britain by Clays Ltd, Elcograf S.p.A.

The paper and board used in this book are made
from wood from responsible sources.

MIX
Paper from
responsible sources
FSC® C104740

Orion Children's Books
An imprint of Hachette Children's Group
Part of Hodder & Stoughton Limited
Carmelite House
50 Victoria Embankment
London EC4Y 0DZ

An Hachette UK Company
www.hachette.co.uk
www.hachettechildrens.co.uk

For all the female scientists whose brilliant work

has been attributed to male colleagues

'Be kind, for everyone you meet is

fighting a hard battle.'

Ian Maclaren

Prologue

7 April 1832

The boy comes out of nowhere, running so fast across the cobblestones that I almost don't see him. And now he is so close that I can smell him. Autumn and the tang of the ocean. Woodsmoke and seaweed. I take a step back to look at him properly. Tall. Black curly hair. Wild blue eyes. Long eyelashes spiked with tiny globes of rain. Pale face twisted in desperation. Horse hooves clatter along the cobbles as a cart weighed down with sacks of flour trundles past, leaving behind a cloud of dust that looks, for a moment, like snow. I shiver. My summer dress is thin and flimsy and lifts above my knees with every gust of damp wind.

He grabs my arm and I flinch. 'Do you know where Anthos is?'

I stare at him, too startled to reply. *How does he know about* Anthos*?*

'It's a ship,' he continues.

'I know,' I say, my throat suddenly dry as toast.

The boy pushes his hand through tight black curls and looks quickly over his shoulder. A trader emerges from the crowd and presents us with a pair of handmade brown leather gloves, his fingers long and thin, his nails blackened with dirt. His eyes are blank, as though he has no expectation from life. His shoulders are hunched, his boots scuffed, his clothes crudely patched. I inhale the sharpness of the new leather, but the boy waves the trader away and scowls. The old man shrugs and limps away.

'That was unkind,' I say.

The boy shrugs. 'You said you know? About *Anthos*?'

Sailors shout instructions at one another even though they have surely loaded sailcloth, rope and twine on to boats a thousand times before. They are barely visible; in the short time since I have been standing here, the rain has eased and a sea fret has descended on the small port. I have been forbidden from coming here and now this strange boy is asking questions I don't want to answer.

I try to make out the names on the hulls of the boats, but the fog only reveals a few letters at a time. A fishing boat called *Sailor's Fright*? No! *Sailor's Delight*. I strain my eyes. Towards the end of the quay is a large vessel, a ship rather than a fishing boat. I can just about make out an 'A'. An 'N'. A 'U'. Or is it a worn-away 'O'?

A foghorn penetrates the air and makes me jump. Not the boy, though. The boy, it seems, knows the sounds of the sea. I want to escape him, but when I step to one side, he does the same, as though we are engaged in a strange dance. A shadow even when there is no sun. A moment of silence follows, in which the sailors take a breath between loads and the carts are piled up with flour just along the quay at Slipper Mill.

Coming here was a mistake. I haven't been to the port in Emsworth since I was a young girl. The boy narrows his eyes. I look over his shoulder and point.

'It's that one, there,' I say.

'You really are stupid if you think I'm falling for that old trick,' he laughs, his lip curling.

I push past with force, forgetting to be scared of him. There, on the smooth cobbles, is a kitten, sitting very still, its tail curled in a perfect semi-circle around its front paws. She must be female; nearly all calico cats are. Her coat is so chaotic that she looks as though she has fallen into successive pots of black, orange and white paint. Her mouth opens and closes, but emits no sound. She looks straight at me and offers a silent *meow*, and my heart somersaults.

'I will call you Astra,' I say. 'You probably don't know this, but "Astra" means star. I have always dreamed of having my own kitten and calling it Astra!'

A hand closes around my arm, but I shake it off. Astra starts to run, galloping down the quay, darting out of the way of sailors and traders. I run after her, past a woman dragging her sobbing son along by the ear, past a thin girl who looks my age, slumped in a doorway, holding out her hand. I pause and reach inside the pocket of my dress: a fossil, a folded-up scrap of newspaper, a lucky four-leaf clover that I carry everywhere and a coin. It is the only money I have, but I press the shilling into her hand and, before she can lift her head, I set off after the kitten again.

A flicker of white fur. I zigzag past all the people milling around the quay. A flash of orange, as though the kitten is flying through the air. I smile; she is running up the wooden gangplank leading to the ship. At the top, she stops. Her green eyes widen, as though challenging me. I turn. No sign of the boy. I put one foot on the gangplank. Then the other. Before I know it, I am aboard *Anthos*.

1

29 February 1832

The snow falls silently to the ground. A sheet of immaculate white. Bobby and Charlie tumble out of the front door and throw themselves on to the snow, squealing at the cold, marvelling at the identical shapes their bodies make in the silvery wonderland. When the light reflects off the many sides of a snowflake, it appears white, but snow is in fact translucent – when my aunt told me that, I couldn't believe it. I think about telling my brothers later, but what's the point? They will only look at each other, raise their eyes to heaven and then stick their tongues out at me.

'Mother,' I say, turning away from the kitchen window, 'if I wrap up warm, may I join the twins? I will be careful not to fall over.'

Mother shakes her head from her place at the kitchen table without bothering to look up. 'Don't you have embroidery to be getting on with, Nico? You'll most certainly catch a cold if you go outside and then who will do your chores? Who will teach the boys this afternoon?'

As my heart sinks, Bobby and Charlie's muffled laughter drifts in with the draught beneath the front door.

'Have you seen my copy of *The Times*?' asks Father, without getting up from his armchair by the fire.

I remember seeing it earlier and dash into the hallway to pull it out of his coat pocket. 'It's here!' I say. He takes it without a word.

'Perhaps I can read one of the articles to you?' I ask.

Father looks over the top of his reading glasses. 'Why on earth would I want you to read to me? I am not a child.'

I bite my lower lip and busy myself by tidying up the twins' mess on the kitchen table. Books and paper, quills and ink. I take a quill, made from a particularly fine goose feather, and pretend to dip it in ink.

'Stop playing, Nico,' says Mother sharply. 'You know full well the quills belong to Bobby and Charlie.'

I nod obediently and put it away.

'Goodness, Ida,' says Father. 'Will you take a look at this!'

Mother gets up, hands planted firmly on her lower back to steady her growing bump. She knows the baby growing inside her is a boy because she tied her wedding ring to a piece of string and it swung back and forth. With me the string swung in a circular motion again and again, no matter how many times Mother tried to make  it swing back and forth. *Oh, the disappointment.*

Mother leans over Father's shoulder. 'Well, I never,' she says, peering at the newspaper article. 'Your sister is finally having a break from her travels. I have to say that is a beautiful drawing of *Anthos*.'

'My sister is a fool,' says Father, closing *The Times* abruptly, and making Mother jump.

I know I am asking for trouble, but I am unable to contain my excitement at news of my favourite aunt. 'What does it say, Father?'

'It's the shortest article you can imagine,' he grunts. 'It barely even counts as news.' Nevertheless, he is unable to resist. He opens the paper again and reads aloud. "'*Dr Hamilton, who recently returned from his* – his! – *successful voyage to Siberia, will set sail again in April. There will doubtless be further vital discoveries made that will change the way we look at the world.*" I can't believe the fool is still dressing up as a man, pretending to be a famous scientist and dilly-dallying about on a boat. This is precisely why women shouldn't be educated!'

I often imagine what it would be like if Aunt were to invite me on board and welcome me into her world of fossils and stars and equations. I don't intend to say a single word out loud, but words tumble out of my mouth before I can stop them. 'I wish I could be a famous scientist just like Aunt Ruth!'

Father's face turns beetroot red. 'You want to be a famous scientist who dresses up as a man, barely spends any time with her husband and doesn't have any children because she sacrificed everything for her work?'

'Yes,' I say boldly. 'I think it's fine for women to have a family *and* a career as a scientist. Maybe Aunt Ruth didn't want children. That's fine too.'

'Enough!' shouts Mother, her face flushed. 'Women are not allowed on ships for good reason. Their place is not at sea, but in the home. Pretending to be a man is preposterous and Ruth shouldn't be allowed to get away with it.' She returns to her seat at the kitchen table, landing with a heavy thud on her chair. 'You will not mention that woman's name again in this house. The only sister we shall acknowledge is Aunt Bertha, who is respectful to your father as well as being a good wife and mother.'

'I miss Aunt Ruth,' I mumble.

'*What* did you say, Nico Cloud?' Father flings the newspaper in the fire and jumps to his feet, waggling his finger at me. 'I too forbid you to mention her name in this house. Go to your room immediately!'

The newspaper crackles furiously but, as I leave the room, I notice the bottom of it is sticking out. There is the drawing of *Anthos*, defiantly refusing to perish. I will sneak downstairs and save it when no one else is around.

'Are you still here?' Mother growls.

I stomp loudly up the wooden stairs. Near the top, I stand and wait, holding my breath.

'I am sorry, Solomon. That girl just doesn't seem to understand her place in this household,' says Mother. 'I have no idea why she thinks she should have an opinion. About anything, never mind your vulgar, bragging sister. The whole situation really is obscene.'

'Nico thinks she's as clever as Ruth, but they are as idiotic as each other,' says Father. There is an ominous silence before he starts speaking again. 'I'm afraid there is only one answer.'

I cover my ears. I don't want to hear. Then again, I need to know their intentions. Even if they won't listen to what I have to say. Because they never, ever listen to me. I lower my hands.

'Are you sure?' asks Mother.

'Yes,' says Father. I know he's prodding at the fire – I can hear the crackle of a new log that hasn't properly dried out. 'We confiscate her maps and her preposterous collection of blasted seeds.' I don't know why Father finds my seeds so infuriating. If he would let me explain then he might understand. He doesn't know what he's missing out on: seeds are everything. Father pauses. 'And we confiscate her books!'

I clap a hand over my mouth to stifle a gasp.

I have two books. I begged Mother and Father to buy them for me every single day for a year. I persuaded them in the end, arguing that I would use them to teach the twins. One is about seeds and fossils – *The A-Z of Seeds and Fossils* – the other about myths and legends: *The Book of Lore and Legends*. As for the maps – Aunt Ruth gave them to me the last time I saw her, when I was seven years old, to illustrate the importance of travel, of seeing the world. And, worst of all, they want to steal my beloved seeds, collected over years and years.

They can't take the things I love the most away from me. My heartbeat is thudding in my ears. I strain to hear.

Father is still talking. '. . . Nico has to learn that no one is remotely interested in what she has to say about acorns or dinosaurs.'

I want to run back downstairs and defend myself. I want to shout and scream at them.

Why can't you love me like you love my stupid brothers?

I don't. Instead, I put my foot on the next stair.

'Did you hear that?' Mother asks.

'It's just the house creaking with the cold,' says Father.

I tiptoe back to my room, pick up the embroidery and stab the needle through the cloth. I wait for Mother to appear at my door and tell me off for earwigging, but the house is silent. I cast aside the embroidery and, for a moment, all I can hear is the icicles dripping outside the window.

The stillness is broken by my brothers' excited yelps drifting through the air as they throw snowballs at each other. Soon they will appear in our bedroom, faces and hands red raw, teeth chattering. Their loud, boisterous voices will fill the room and Mother will laugh at everything they say while I sit silently on my bed and finish off embroidering the pink rose that I've been working on for months. I sigh dramatically. It feels good and so I do it again.

But I will not cry.

*

I stand on my thin, hard bed and look at all the books on the bookshelf. I remember how excited I was when Father told me that the word science was from the Latin word *'scientia'*, meaning 'knowledge'. Back then,

I stupidly believed that he would allow me to go to school with the twins. Instead, I give them extra lessons after school and at the weekend, in between other chores and yet more embroidery. And the last time Father talked of science was years ago, long before Aunt Ruth became successful and he became so angry.

It suddenly becomes clear that I must not only hide my favourite things but that, when the time is right, I must leave home. If only for the day. I need to know that Mother and Father will miss me once they notice I have gone. Perhaps then they will think twice about confiscating my things.

There are a dozen books on the shelf, only two of them mine. I take down *The Book of Lore and Legends* and *The A-Z of Seeds and Fossils*, but the spaces between the remaining books look like the gaps between the twins' teeth, so I put them back.

Maybe, though, there's something I can do about

the maps. There's a large cloth bag on the back of the
bedroom door, decorated with a puffin. It probably

won't be missed.
It was not my
finest attempt at
embroidery; the
bird's beak is
dark purple and
not bright
orange because

that was the cheapest thread in the shop. I hide the map
of Europe that Aunt Ruth gave me in the bag. As I fold
it, I see fragments of France, Spain, Italy, Corsica,
Sardinia and Sicily and I sigh. I will never see those
countries. I'll probably never leave England. Or even
Sussex. But I fold the map of Europe until it can be
folded no more, hoping the paper doesn't rip.

There's the box too, shoved right under my bed and

tied with several ribbons so that I will immediately know if Bobby or Charlie have been snooping around. I hold my breath and listen for the sound of footsteps on the stairs. Nothing. The twins have probably built a snowman by now, with a long carroty nose and mean raisin eyes, and no doubt my father's pipe stuck into its pretend mouth.

I take the trilobite fossil carefully out of the box. It might look like a flattened woodlouse, but it's a sea creature that lived hundreds of millions of years ago.

Also in the box, hidden beneath an old copy of *The Times*, is my grandmother's jet brooch. A rose is intricately carved into the black wood. Jet is a fossil that was created when the wood from a monkey puzzle tree washed out to sea in the Triassic period (over 200 million years ago, which is so hard to imagine that it makes my head hurt, but it's exciting too because it's when dinosaurs roamed). I decide to add the brooch to the puffin bag as a reminder of my warm, kind grandma, who would surely be turning in her grave if she knew how cruel my father had become.

I don't want to think about Father, so I rifle in the box till I find my paper bags of seeds. In one bag there are dark brown acorns, with strange scaly cupules that look like little hats; and in another the dried-out flowerhead of the milk thistle, whose small brown seeds are attached to white parachutes. There are cloth bags full of stripy black and white sunflower seeds, wrinkled horse chestnuts and the Norway maple seeds that flutter to the ground like green insects.

I pick a few favourites and fill a small cloth bag: brown beech seeds, kidney-shaped poppy seeds, the yellow kernels of sweet corn, salad leaf seeds, radish, red pepper, spinach, beans and sweet peas. And, as an afterthought, brown beech seeds and the horse chestnuts. I might meet someone who needs them.

Right at the bottom of the box, is my notebook. I open it, savouring the smell of its leather covers. I remember how excited I was when Aunt Ruth gave me my very own notebook – before Father decided she was a bad influence on me and her visits came to an abrupt halt. I was convinced that I'd fill every page with wise thoughts and intricate drawings. The first page is just a handful of words, written in an elaborate script as though I was half-hoping somebody might find the notebook and say that I could be a scientist straight away, at the age of seven.

I hold the page up to the light coming in from the window: *Fossils are the past, but seeds are the future.*

I believe that now more than ever.

On the second page is a drawing that took me hours

and hours to complete, but that I had forgotten about: the legendary Tree of Hope.

It's from my favourite page in *The Book of Lore and Legends*. I would turn to that page whenever I was sent to my room to think about speaking out of turn, or speaking at all. Soon, as if by magic, I would forget I was in a small bedroom in Sussex, and be transported back thousands of years to a field of olive trees in Sicily, feeling the dusty heat on my skin.

According to *The Book of Lore and Legends*, there was once a sacred tree in the middle of a field in Sicily. It had a gnarly, knotted trunk so thick that two people with outstretched arms couldn't manage to reach the tips of each other's fingers. The so-called Tree of Hope had the same silvery-green leaves as the army of olive trees that protected it, but, instead of producing olives that turned slowly from green to black as they ripened, it was covered in bright red fruit all year round.

The deep red fruit was round like an apple, but slightly larger, and so heavy that the branches of the tree creaked with its weight. One by one, the fruit would split open to reveal dazzling red seeds that shone like precious stones. Birds gorged themselves on its treasure. On occasion a solitary bird would visit that none of the locals recognised. A large bird, too heavy to fly very far, it was nicknamed the *briccone*, Italian for 'rascal'.

The *briccone* had the vibrant plumage of a peacock. Its neck was bright blue, its feathers shimmering blue and green. Its eyes were tiny, its beak large and curved, its claws ugly and sharp. It fought other birds for the shiny red seeds.

Local Sicilians both respected and feared the tree. Some thought it must be haunted by demons – or that the *briccone* was itself a demon – because how else could the tree bear its bright fruit when frost hardened the ground? Other locals crept through the field at night and took handfuls of seeds from the gaping fruit, wiping their reddened hands on their aprons. When their bodies ached or they had little food to feed their family, they secretly beat the seeds to a pulp and hid it in soups and smiled to themselves when the aches disappeared and their tummies stopped rumbling. Yet they didn't dare plant the seeds and grow their own Tree of Hope for fear of being scorned by the other locals.

No one knows what happened to the tree – or, indeed, if it ever existed. I have always liked to think it did.

I smile at my drawing of the Tree of Hope and put the leather notebook at the bottom of the puffin bag.

The wardrobe is stuffed full of my brothers' immaculate shirts and trousers. My dresses, all of which have seen better days, are squashed to one side. I take the thinnest, lightest one as it will be easier to carry.

The icicles are still dripping as they rapidly melt, but the twins aren't making a racket any more. They must have come back inside. I put the dress on top of the seeds, the map, the ancient sea creature and grandmother's brooch at the bottom of the bag.

There is a bundle of the twins' clothes at the bottom of the wardrobe, waiting to be worn again by the new baby, and I hide the puffin bag underneath it. As soon as I am able, I will leave for the day.

'*Fossils are the past, but seeds are the future,*' I whisper to myself as I climb into bed.

2

6 April 1832

Tomorrow is the day.

Alone in the room I share with the twins, I sit on my bed, my legs swinging back and forth. My brothers' laughter drifts up the stairs — they are no doubt being tickled by Father. I get up and push the door shut, loudly enough to give myself some satisfaction, but not loudly enough to be heard by anyone else. I open the wardrobe. My bag is still there, beneath the baby clothes.

I glance up at the bookshelf where *The Book of Lore and Legends* and *The A-Z of Fossils and Seeds* used to sit, before they were confiscated. I pull the petals off a dried dandelion from last summer that I flattened in one of the twins' books.

They will miss me.

They will miss me not.

They will miss me.

They will miss me not.

I unfold the piece of newspaper I keep under my mattress, rescued when everyone else was sleeping. The edges are charred by fire, but I can still see the drawing of *Anthos*, her sails billowing in the wind. I trace the headline with my index finger: *ANTHOS WILL SET SAIL AGAIN 7th APRIL 1832.*

I have to catch a glimpse of Aunt Ruth's boat before it sets sail, even if it's from afar. I have to believe that another life exists. And perhaps Mother and Father really will miss me.

'It is time,' I whisper. 'It's now or never.'

3

7 April 1832

'Who are you?'

The voice is full of impatience and irritation. I pull the map off my face. It's a boy's voice but I can't see his face; I can't see a thing. The fog is so dense that it feels solid, as though you could push it away with your hands. My heart clatters in my chest. I reach down until my hand touches the puffin bag. Thank goodness it's still there.

It takes a second to work out where I am. I remember sitting down in the rowing boat secured to one side of the deck on *Anthos* with the kitten in my arms and then . . . I must have fallen asleep. I throw off the damp blanket, sit up quickly. *What if it's the boy from the quay?*

Whoever it is jabs at the boat until it gently sways. The sharp smell of varnish stains my nostrils. I stretch out my arms and hold on to the boat's wooden sides. They are smooth but still slightly sticky. I don't think I can stand up.

'I asked you a question,' he says.

He shoves the boat again, more forcefully this time. My stomach lurches.

My lips are dry, but I must find my voice.

'I am Nico Cloud, sir,' I say.

The boat comes to a rest. A lantern shoots out of the fog, attached to a ghostly hand.

'How old are you, Nico Cloud?'

Should I lie and pretend I am older? Probably best not to. If I lie, I will have to remember the lie.

'I just turned twelve,' I say quietly.

'Why are you on *this* ship, hiding in *this* rowing boat?'

'I wasn't hiding. I fell asleep,' I say, folding my map up quickly. 'Obviously it was a mistake. The falling asleep, I mean. I saw a gorgeous kitten run on to *Anthos* and then jump into this rowing boat. I followed her and dropped off. Anyway, I must take my leave now or

Mother and Father will notice my absence and I will no doubt be locked in my room for days or given endless boring chores or . . . I only left home for the day to see if my parents would miss me. They only seem to have eyes for my annoying twin brothers. And Mother has another boy on the way . . .'

I always talk quickly when I'm anxious. And, most of the time, I regret it.

I try to stand up, but the ground beneath my feet feels like it's moving and I end up back where I started, on my bottom.

'You won't be able to stand up because you haven't got your sea legs yet! Did you not hear the ship's anchor being pulled up?' asks the voice. He steps closer and I see that it is a boy, a small smile forming on his lips as he holds the lantern close to my face.

The fog is silently fading. The boy puts the lantern down and I squint at him in the bright sunlight. I see immediately that it's not the same boy from before. This one is tall and thin, with sharp corners. He has grown too tall for his trousers and his small shirt clings awkwardly to his torso. His eyes are blue and his ears stick out of his light brown hair, as though his mother dangled him from both his ears for fun when he was young. I smile at the thought. *Can I trust him?*

Beyond him the land is fading as fast as the fog and the brilliant blue sea is glittering in the sun.

'We're moving,' I say, feeling numb. 'We're at sea.' *I am in such trouble.*

'What's that noise?' he asks, staring at my puffin bag. It's the kitten, scratching and mewling inside.

'I didn't catch *your* name,' I say loudly, to distract him. 'You must have a name. And an age.'

'I do,' the boy asks, raising an eyebrow. 'I'm Matteo and yes, I do in fact have an age – nearly fourteen. Why are you here on *Anthos*?'

'It was a mistake,' I say again.

'Never mind,' he says. 'You are here and we have set sail. We are heading east and then we shall head north, towards Scotland. I suggest you hide somewhere less obvious than this rowing boat. I'll take you down to the bread room. I'm the only one who uses flour, so you should be safe there for now.'

I gather myself. *My aunt must be on this ship*, I think.

Before I can say anything, an older man's voice shouts from the other end of the ship. 'Matteo?'

'Give me your hand,' Matteo says. 'We must be quick. No one can see you. Leave your bag, I'll get it later.'

'I can't,' I say, picking up the straps and taking his warm, rough hand in mine. 'Everything I have is inside this bag. Maps and seeds and fossils and an extra summer dress.'

'Oh! An extra dress?'

'I was running away,' I explain. 'But only for the day.'

'And now,' says Matteo, his voice dropping to a whisper as he guides me along the deck of the ship. 'Now you have become an accidental stowaway.'

4

Matteo pushes me gently into the bread room, which is packed full of sacks of flour and lined with silver. It feels claustrophobic and chilly after the tantalising glimpse of the blueness of the sea and the sky. I sit down on a half-empty sack of flour and look around at the silver walls.

'We had to cover the walls with tin to deter rats,' he explains.

I shudder at the thought of those creatures hotfooting it all around me.

Matteo eases the lid off a small chest using the tips of

his fingers – his nails are bitten to the quick – and hands me a biscuit with tiny holes in it.

'Here, have this,' he says, smiling broadly, as if he's bestowing me a feast. As he leans forward, I catch a whiff of him: seaweed and salt and fish and smoke. It's strangely comforting.

I break off a tiny bit of biscuit. It's so dry that it's an effort not to spit it out into the hem of my dress. When he sees my face, he scowls. 'The ship's biscuit is a treat. There's barley, rye *and* bean flour in there.'

'Thank you,' I say, wrapping the biscuit in my handkerchief and putting it in my bag. 'I'll save it for later. I don't mean to be rude, I'm just not very hungry just now.'

'I am needed elsewhere,' he says, and starts backing out of the bread room. He stares at me for a moment, as though to confirm that I am indeed real. 'I'll check on you later.'

Without thinking, I say, 'When you have a moment, can you tell my Aunt Ruth that I'm here?'

'Your aunt?' he asks, looking confused. My stomach lurches; I have made a terrible mistake.

'I am still half-asleep,' I tell him. 'I was thinking of the aunt I intended to visit in Emsworth – I forgot that I am trapped here for the time being. This ship is called *Anthos*, isn't it?'

'Indeed it is,' says Matteo, pulling at an ear.

'"*Anthos*" is Greek for flower . . .'

Matteo narrows his eyes, but his voice is not unkind. 'Well, I have never been to Greece. I am sure you know that women have been forbidden aboard ships since 1808. That is why you must leave as soon as possible. I imagine girls such as yourself are even more . . .'

He pauses to think of the right word.

'Outlawed? Forbidden? Taboo?'

'Yes, all of those things,' says Matteo quietly. 'They

are not my rules.'

'They are very unfair rules,' I say.

'I agree. But even so, you will have to disembark when we next drop anchor,' he says, his hand on the door handle. 'If I don't go now, someone will come looking for me here and you will be caught and made to walk the plank.'

I can't tell if he's joking.

'Wait!' I say. 'Please. Is there a scientist on board?'

Matteo nods. 'Of course. We are in the service of Doctor Hamilton. He is one of the world's leading scientists.'

She is here, then, I think with relief.

I notice a cheeky paw pushing at the cloth of my bag so I pull it closer, covering it with my hand.

'I won't lock you in and you can keep my lantern,' says Matteo, 'but please don't wander around the ship – and don't go down the stairs that lead to the black door. I was joking about walking the plank, but the captain could punish you for boarding the ship without permission. It's not his style, mind you – I'm just saying he *could*. We would most definitely keep your cat, though. Useful for keeping the rats under control.'

'You know that I kept Astra after following her on to *Anthos*?'

Matteo smiles, his eyes bright. 'Well, I might not be a Greek scholar, but I notice everything.'

*

With Matteo gone, the cabin suddenly feels quiet, even though I was doing most of the talking. I take Astra by the scruff of the neck and lift her out of the cloth bag. I slowly lean back against the tin wall and place her on my chest. Her tiny black, white and ginger body vibrates with a loud, insistent purr. She lies flat against my body, her paws stretched up towards my shoulders, her head nuzzled into my neck. She buffs my chin with her wet nose and promptly falls asleep again.

'It's your fault I ended up being a stowaway,' I say, kissing her wet nose and placing her carefully on another sack of flour. 'I hope you're grateful for my company at least.'

I take a deep breath. Here in the bread room, where I am separated from the water only by wood and tin, I can feel the ship pushing through the waves, taking me further and further away from Mother, Father and the twins.

'This ship will be my new home,' I tell Astra, who is now snoring gently and who certainly doesn't seem to care where she lives as long as it's warm.

*

The lantern tilts suddenly to one side, turning the tinplated ceiling from silver to white. I stand up with some difficulty, then tumble against the opposite wall. The lantern crashes to the ground and plunges the room into darkness.

'No need to panic, Astra. I've got this.'

I manage to locate the leather notebook and Grandma's brooch in my bag, put them in the pocket of my dress and then feel my way along the wall until I find the door handle. I open the door just enough to see outside. The sun is beginning to fade. It must already be mid-afternoon. Two men are shouting instructions at one another at the other end of the ship, but otherwise no one appears to be around. I can't see Matteo anywhere.

If I can find Aunt Ruth, I'm pretty sure I'll be safe.

'I'll be back soon, Astra, don't worry,' I say, kissing her tiny head. I step gingerly outside the door. I don't want to risk being caught and I certainly don't want to have to walk the plank. I am an excellent swimmer, but the sea will be freezing and . . . I don't even want to think about it. But Matteo can't expect me to just sit in the darkness and wait for him. It's too much like being back in my room, with my needle and thread. Not that he would understand that.

The stairs from the bread room are wet and slippery, but somehow I make it to the deck. A boy is ascending the mast at breakneck speed, his hands and legs moving in a blur. The white sails ripple in the breeze. Without warning, two men appear on deck. I run to the side of the ship and crouch down, hiding in the shadows of the rowing boat. What did Aunt once tell me about the different words that are used on a ship? If I am facing the bow of the ship, as I am, port is left and starboard is right. So I'm on the starboard side.

When I can no longer see legs rushing backwards and forwards, I slowly stand up. My dress is damp from the sea spray, but I have to press on.

I walk to the middle of the ship without being seen,

and locate another flight of stairs that lead to a black door. If Matteo forbade me from going near it, there must be a good chance it's Aunt's cabin.

I check behind me – no one is there. I walk quickly down the steps. At the bottom, I find a wooden door and put my ear against it, but can't hear a thing. I push the handle down and open the door just a crack.

My heart beats faster. I am expecting someone to jump out and say, 'Who goes there?' but the room appears to be empty. A small, round porthole window flecked with salt allows light to stream into the room and I can see the sparkling sea through it. The wallpaper is strange; as I walk up close to it, I see why. It's not wallpaper at all, but sheet upon sheet of paper attached to the wall. And on the paper, endless mathematical equations and diagrams and intricate illustrations of fossils.

I gasp and immediately clamp my hand over my mouth for fear of drawing attention to myself.

I trace the illustrations on the cabin wall with my fingers. This is exactly how I once decorated the wall next to my bed. I carefully nailed my pencil drawings of fossils and seeds to the wall and lay in bed staring at them, learning their Latin names off by heart. Until one day I returned to my room to discover every single sheet of paper torn down and scrunched up into balls. Bobby and Charlie swore it wasn't them, but who else might have done such a thing?

There's a faint smell of tobacco in the air, a desk littered with yet more paper and a metal trunk with a big lock. A small table adjacent to the desk is covered with a faded tablecloth. I tentatively lift a corner and see a row of empty glass vials and a box of soil underneath.

This must be Aunt Ruth's room.

The door creaks open.

'*Who* on earth are you and *what* on earth do you think you are you doing here, in my private cabin? I only

56

popped out for a second.'

I spin round and stand in front of the small table, my hands behind my back, my face hot with guilt. A short man is glaring at me, his cheeks flushed. He appears muscular beneath his bright blue shirt and yet his shoulders are surprisingly narrow. My heart beats faster. *Please don't make me walk the plank!*

Surely this isn't Aunt Ruth? She was so much taller

than me last time I saw her.

The man's dark hair is dishevelled. I notice it's the same colour as mine, and there's something familiar about his eyes. Deep grey eyes behind large glasses. His suit doesn't fit very well, the tweed trousers are too long, the matching jacket too tight.

'I don't have time to repeat myself,' he says, quickly shuffling the paper scattered around the desk into neat piles. 'Tell me, now. Who are you and what are you doing here?'

'I was looking for Dr H . . . H . . . Hamilton.'

'And so you have found Dr Hamilton.'

I swallow hard. 'Aunt Ruth? It's me, Nico. Nico Cloud.'

Dr Hamilton looks blankly at me. This was not what I was expecting. This Aunt Ruth is not like the kindly aunt I remember.

'I am your niece, Nico. Your brother is my father. I'm his daughter. You're my aunt.' I take the leather notebook and the brooch out of my pocket. 'You gave me this leather notebook when I was seven. And a map of Europe. This is Grandma's jet brooch. Do you remember? I brought it for you.'

My aunt takes the brooch, stares at it for a moment and then places it carefully on her desk. 'Nico?' she says, taking off her glasses and rubbing at her eyes. 'How did you find your way on to *Anthos*? Is that *really* you?' Her face softens and she instantly looks more familiar. 'But you were this high when we last met' – she indicates somewhere around the height of her mid-thigh – 'I never stopped to think that you'd be so grown up by now.'

Dizzy with relief that my aunt remembers me, I step forward and offer my hand, leaning in to inhale her smell. Tobacco, ink, earth, something sharp and the tang of salt, like Matteo. She takes a moment to shake my hand, but I don't mind – she hasn't pushed me away like Mother and Father do when I get close to them. Then she pats me on the shoulder a few times as though I am a semi-feral animal that needs to be soothed. I stand awkwardly in the middle of the room as Aunt sits down at her desk and lights her pipe.

'Is that good for you, Aunt? It's such a . . .' – how not to be rude – 'distinctive smell.'

'Well, in the 1570s tobacco was thought to relieve almost every ailment you could think of, from toothache to bad breath, from worms to lockjaw. But I agree, the smell is rather foul until you're used to it.' She puts her pipe down on a plate decorated with puffins clustered tightly together on a rock.

'Aunt! I have a bag decorated with a puffin! The puffin isn't quite right, but . . .'

'You love puffins too? That's excellent news. Puffins are otherwise known as—'

'Sea parrots! And their beak changes colour according to the season. And they can live for twenty years!'

'Very good, Nico,' says Aunt, looking a little bemused.

She looks over the top of her thick-rimmed glasses. 'Nico, I must ask . . . *Why* are you here, on *Anthos*?'

I understand that my answer must be short or Aunt will lose interest. She is clearly busy so there certainly isn't time to tell her that I left home at dawn this morning, shocked by how cold it was before the sun came up and momentarily distracted by the silvery clouds that formed each time I exhaled. Or how, at the end of our road, I felt for my favourite fossil in the pocket of my dress and quickly opened the bag to check my precious belongings were still inside, half-hoping that by delaying, Mother or Father would come dashing out of the house and beg me to stay.

Or that I had to walk for hours to reach the dock, just to see if *Anthos* was moored there. The ship's deck had been sluiced down with salt water and was sparkling in the sun, making it slippery. I slid this way and that before managing *finally* to catch Astra by the scruff of the neck when she climbed into the rowing boat. I sat down for a rest and didn't even know I'd fallen asleep until Matteo found us.

'Nico?' asks Aunt, impatiently tapping her pipe on the puffin plate.

I was daydreaming again. 'Sorry. Why am I here? I want to see the world,' I say. I daren't tell her that I want to be scientist in case she laughs at me. She's a real scientist, after all.

She looks away from me, out of the porthole to the vastness of the ocean. 'I'm afraid you won't see much of the world on *Anthos*. I am exhausted – my crew and I recently returned from a long, difficult voyage to Siberia a month ago. As you can see from those.' She waves vaguely at the maps above her desk, which have pins dotted over the vast expanse of land stretching from the Ural Mountains to the borders of Mongolia and China.

'Wow! What did you find in Siberia?'

'Stone tools. Bone fragments. Mammoth tusks. The usual.'

'Will you ever return to Siberia, Aunt?'

'Unlikely. I had to sell some of my paintings just to fund this trip round the British coast.' She turns back towards me and looks wistful for a moment. 'Never mind. We just have to ensure we are not plundered. Time is not on our side. The clock does not stop simply because we want it to.'

My mind races. I am pretty sure that only pirates plunder at sea. 'Pirates! Are they closing in on us?'

Aunt raises one eyebrow. 'Don't worry yourself, Nico. As I say, you won't see the world on this trip. I suggest you disembark when we get close enough to land. Etienne – a young lad in my crew – can take you ashore in the rowing boat. You will, of course, have to find your own way home. I cannot be responsible for your welfare, Nico.

That's my brother's job.'

I can't go back to Father – he will no doubt be glad I have gone. When I left the house this morning, I slammed the front door loudly behind me. Not once, but twice. No one came after me. No one cares. The realisation is painful, but it simply spurs me on.

'But, Aunt . . . I want to learn everything there is to know about science.'

'Go on,' she says, leaning back in her chair and relighting her pipe. 'I will grant you a few minutes of my time, no more.'

'I want you to teach me everything you know. About the way fossils preserve life for thousands of years. About minerals turning old bones and tusks and shells into stones . . .'

Aunt Ruth gets up from her chair and stands in front of me, her arms crossed. 'So you want to be a paleontologist – a scientist who specialises in the study of ancient life.'

'Yes! Well, no. I'm interested in seeds above anything else. Do you think we can look at the past and the future at the same time?'

'I don't see why not. Tell me, why the fascination with seeds?'

I sense that this is my last chance, my only chance, to persuade Aunt not to throw me off *Anthos* at the earliest opportunity. This is what I have been waiting for my whole life: a chance to show what I know, to share my knowledge with someone who cares about the same things as me. With someone who could teach me everything I dream of learning.

I look at all the maps and diagrams and illustrations on the walls around us, cocooning us with facts about the natural world, and take another deep breath. 'I have collected dozens and dozens of seeds. Perhaps hundreds. Capsules, which are just pods really, change from green to brown or from black to red and then they open and the seeds blow away. So I have to collect seeds as soon as the pods ripen. The birds like to gorge on fleshy berries, so I have to be quick with those too . . .

'As you know, not all seeds look the same. Orchids have delicate seeds like dust. Others I can bash with a stone and nothing happens because their husks are completely impenetrable. But we can't live without either. We are nothing without seeds, Aunt.'

She sighs and takes her seat once again. I can't stop now. 'We depend on plants for every breath of air we take and every mouthful of food we eat. Sometimes I can't sleep at night because I worry that Earth is heading for its sixth mass extinction. The last extinction was around 66 million years ago, when an asteroid hit Earth and *boom!* – all the dinosaurs were killed. But it gave mammals and birds the chance to evolve.'

'I'm listening,' she says, putting her pipe down.

I push my hand into my pocket and close my fist

around the soft contours of the trilobite fossil. 'I've read my book about seeds and fossils at least a hundred times. Sometimes seeds and fossils cross over, like the cross pollination in flowers, I suppose, when pollen from the male part of the flower is transferred to the female part. You know about cross pollination . . .'

'Yes, thank you.'

'Of course. Sorry.' I swallow hard. *Keep going.* 'But the thing is that there are actual fossils of flowering plants, Aunt. They date back 130 million years. Which makes them older than dinosaurs, which disappeared at the end of the Cretaceous period, around 101 to 66 million years ago. I would love to see the bones of those late Cretaceous dinosaurs. Can you imagine watching a Barosaurus from behind a bush?' I pause for breath.

There's a glimmer of a smile on Aunt's face. 'I wouldn't recommend hiding behind a bush, given the Barosaurus' herbivorous diet. They might take a bite of the bush and out of your bottom at the same time.'

Is she making a joke?

I can feel the excitement rushing around my body, making my arms and legs tingle. 'True! You can see the grasses they ate in their fossilised poo. And you can see the seeds of the fruit they ate in the poo too.'

'Fossilised dung, Nico.'

'Yes, Aunt. Dung, not poo. Of course. Sorry.'

'Tell me what your mother and father make of your fascination with science.'

'They find me extremely . . . peculiar.' I look at the ground. 'And Father likes to pretend he's only got one sister. Boring Aunt Bertha.'

Aunt Ruth pulls a face, as though she has just tasted something bitter. 'Bertha is as sharp as a belemnite fossil.'

'I have seen drawings of belemnite fossils, Aunt! I know their soft, squid-like bodies didn't really fossilise, but the guard at the tip of their squishy bodies is super hard so they sometimes survive longer than other fossils. I read that they are quite easy to find on certain beaches.'

'You have been busy, Nico,' says Aunt Ruth. She looks at me for a moment, her shirt bringing out the blue in her grey eyes. 'I could only afford a skeleton crew of four sailors, including the captain, so you will be of some practical use until we next drop anchor. You may stay until then. But when it is time for you to leave, you must go without question, do you hear? I will alert the crew to your attendance on board the ship. We don't want the captain making you walk the plank. Oh and, Nico, tell *no one* that I am your aunt. Or a woman.'

I nod furiously. 'I promise.'

'Now please leave, I have work to be getting on with.'

I shut the door quietly behind me. The lock clicks a second later. I look up at the steep wooden stairs stained with Siberian salt and the flawless blue sky above,

69

interrupted only by the circling seagulls, their bellies as white as chalk, and I make my ascent.

*

My eyes are shut, but I cannot sleep. My body is heavy with exhaustion, but my brain is racing, on high alert because this is my first night away from home. I try not to think of my own bed, with its familiar smell; I am lucky, I tell myself, that there was a spare cabin for me to sleep in for a few nights.

The hammock sways gently from side to side, then it swings violently without warning. My stomach grumbles and bile rises in my throat. *Is this what sea sickness feels like?* The hammock steadies and I shiver. The stove that Matteo lit an hour or so earlier takes the edge off the chill in the cabin, but even with several scratchy blankets covering me I can't seem to get warm. Astra lies next to me, purring so loudly that I can barely hear the wind. I place her on top of my chest to try and retain some heat.

The chunk of bread Matteo gave me for supper hasn't helped with the sickness.

But I'd rather feel sick and hungry all day and all night than go home.

I stare up at the ceiling and think. Aunt Ruth said she has no time for me. Matteo is trying to be kind, but he cannot help me.

If I am sent home, I will be punished.

I will have to promise to teach the twins arithmetic and science and not to talk about Eocene angiosperm while cleaning out the fireplace at dawn. When I tried to explain to Mother that 'Eocene' refers to the geological period dating back 55 million years ago, while 'angiosperm' is a flowering plant that protects its seeds inside a fruit, she sent me to my room for the rest of the day, with nothing to eat or drink. My tummy was grumpy, but I didn't mind too much; while I was sitting on my hard, thin bed, I learned that angiosperm seeds are often found inside a fleshy fruit that birds and animals love to eat and then the seeds are dispersed in the bird and animal poo. *No, not poo, DUNG. Sorry, Aunt Ruth!*

I sigh so hard that Astra opens one eye and peeks up at me.

Oh no. Astra! Mother and Father hate everything with four legs. I can never take her home.

'Nothing to worry about,' I say, more to myself than her, kissing her tiny head.

At least I don't feel as desperate as that boy on the quay this morning. Now that I have remembered him, I can't get his face out of my mind. Perhaps he was scared of something. His curly hair, his delicate eyelashes, his desperate eyes. I shouldn't have run off. I wish I could talk to him and ask him what he wanted from me, but I'll probably never see him again. I might never see Aunt Ruth again after tomorrow. I shouldn't have presumed she'd want to see me again. I remind her of a life she once had, not the one she has now.

My brain buzzes.

The boy on the dock. Aunt Ruth's study. The maps on the wall. The sea fret, fog so thick I couldn't see my own hand. The girl begging for money. Astra flying through the air. Boats looming out of the mist. I can see an 'A'. An 'N'. An 'M'. Why an 'M'? There is no 'M' in Anthos! The begging girl is joined by a dozen other girls and boys, all holding their hands out. Their faces are hollow with hunger. A woman leans down towards them, her hands full of . . . of what? Something golden. But her white dress is stained red.

I wake up with a jolt.

Astra is purring and snoring gently at the same time. For a few minutes I am too scared to go back to sleep, to fall into another bad dream. I name every fossil I can think of, every star I know. I listen to Astra.

purr buzz purr buzz purr buzz purr buzz zz zz

And finally I fall into a deep, dreamless sleep.

73

5

8 April 1832

When I awaken, the cabin is dark, the hammock is swinging wildly from side to side and my tummy is rumbling, almost as loudly as Astra's purr.

With some difficulty, I pull myself out of the hammock and try to stand up. My legs wobble like jelly. Standing up straight is impossible, so I get back on to my hands and knees and crawl towards the door. Astra is hiding beneath the hammock, her body in the shape of a loaf. She is not purring. She is not happy.

The door won't open. I wrench the handle down and

pull it towards me. One. Two. Three. It opens slightly, but then a gust of wind slams it shut again and I'm thrown back inside the cabin. I turn sideways, square my shoulders and push the door with the side of my body with all my might. The door opens and I squeeze through the gap before the vicious wind can trap me inside again. As soon as I step outside, a spray of salty water hits me in the face and I have to wipe my eyes with the back of my hand before I can get my bearings.

It's morning. The sky is filled with furious black clouds, but beyond them lies a promising line of bright blue on the horizon. The storm clouds are coming towards us at speed and *Anthos* is being tossed about in the sea like a child flinging a toy ship around in the bath.

I wonder if Mother has had her baby . . .

'Matteo?' I shout. But his name is whisked away by the wind. I might as well be shouting underwater. Perhaps I should go back and get Astra. I can't bear to think of her sliding across the cabin floor, with nowhere safe to hide. I hope she's not hurt. But then I remember the way her body flew through the air at the port with such little effort and I realise that she will be fine.

A vast wave washes over the deck. I don't know what to do. My first time on a ship, my first storm. I can't see Matteo or the captain – or, indeed, anyone. A boy about the same age as Matteo runs across the deck, slipping and sliding. Perhaps this is Etienne. He is shouting the same four words over and over. 'Batten down the hatches!'

Through the thick rain I can still just about see him, slamming a hatch on the deck tightly shut and securing it with a piece of wood. I tuck my dress in my knickers and follow the boy, but before I know it, he is halfway up the mast. I hold on to the side of the rowing boat with both hands, determined not to let the wind whip me off the deck and into the furious, churning sea. My legs can barely hold me up. I feel breathless. I have never been so

completely exposed to the elements before.

I suddenly long for home. For dry land. Or am I just scared? I wanted an adventure, didn't I?

I decide to knock on Aunt Ruth's door. I don't want to be alone and Ruth is family, after all. So I skid across the deck on my hands and knees, holding on to anything secure. I burn my palms on a length of rope and cling to a coil of rusting metal. I bump down the stairs to Aunt's cabin on my bottom, pull myself up to full height and knock on the door. Nothing. I knock again.

I think I can hear the sound of a key being turned, but the door doesn't open. I knock again, this time with both fists. Seawater flies down the stairs and whacks me with such force that I struggle to catch my breath.

'Dr Hamilton! Aunt! Please let me in!'

The door opens and a hand drags me inside.

'Nico! You are soaking wet. Here, dry yourself with this and sit by the fire.'

I take the warm towel and sit as close to the stove as I dare. How funny to think that, not so long ago, Father threw his copy of *The Times* in the fire after reading about *Anthos* and here I am, on *Anthos*.

'I would offer to lend you some of my clothes,' says Aunt, sitting down. 'But I only have shirts and suits.'

'Aunt?' I stop rubbing my hair with the towel and look up at her. The ship lurches and I have to swallow hard to stop myself from being sick.

'Yes, Nico?'

'I don't want to be rude, but . . . why do you have to pretend to be a man? Is it only while you are on board *Anthos* or do you have to dress as a man when you are working at the university as well? I bet Uncle Raymond never has to pretend to be a woman!'

Aunt laughs and I let out a sigh of relief. 'So many questions!' she says. 'There are several complicated answers, in which I could bore you with all the details of my life as a female scientist. I should start by saying that Uncle is wonderfully supportive, but it's hard for him to see how much I have to compromise to get my work done. I partly dress as a man on board *Anthos* because I don't want anyone to know I'm doing research on here.'

'Why is it so hard to be a female scientist?'

'Science is very much a man's world. For example, I was forced to carry out my research in a dusty old shed on the university campus because women aren't welcome in the science department. Male scientists often tell me how much they respect my work and then they publish it under their own names. No one thinks I should be properly paid, which meant I could barely afford to go to Siberia, never mind make this more local trip.'

I stare at her, open-mouthed. I have no idea what to say, which is pretty rare for me.

Aunt continues. 'I have been able to publish my work as Dr Hamilton, but of course everyone assumes it's my husband. I can see you are shocked, child. All I can say is that I would think very carefully about pursuing your dream of becoming a scientist. Think of the lengths you would have to go to. Why do you think I work on *Anthos*?'

'So that you can drop anchor at beaches and search for fossils?'

Aunt laughs again. 'It would be far easier and cheaper to access the beach by horse and cart. No. I am here because I can work in peace, undisturbed. There are no meddlesome men who want to know my business. So long as Matteo and Etienne remain alert and keep an eye out for other boats, I am much better off in this cabin.'

'Other boats?'

Aunt pauses. I am pretty sure she is wondering if she can trust me.

'It would be easy for someone to steal . . . to report me to the authorities,' she says carefully. 'As you pointed out, women have been forbidden aboard ships for some time. But I don't want my gravestone to read, "She cooked fancy meals for her husband." I'd rather *his* gravestone said that he cooked fancy meals for *me*.'

I try to imagine Father cooking for Mother. I can't. 'Where is Uncle Raymond?'

'Right now? At home, waiting to hear if I have yet had a serious breakthrough.'

'A breakthrough?' This must have something to do with the empty vials and the soil! My whole body feels as though it's full of jumping beans. If I can find a way to stay on *Anthos*, I might even be able to witness the breakthrough . . .

But she simply relights the pipe and puffs out such foul-smelling smoke that I take a step backwards. 'I really must get on. The storm has almost passed. You should change out of that wet dress, assuming you have a spare. Now if you will excuse me.'

I leave her cabin as quietly as I can, a huge smile on my face even though Aunt told me rather rudely to leave. It doesn't matter; she can help me navigate the world of science as a young woman and that means everything.

*

As I am heading back to my cabin to change, I see Matteo standing at the prow of the ship, hands on his hips, elbows jutting out. He looks indignant, as though saying, 'How dare you!' to the storm, even as it eases.

'Matteo!' I shout, untucking my dress from my knickers. 'I survived the storm!'

I can almost see the words fizzing in front of me, like a rabble of bees dizzy on the nectar of a lavender bush. I run across the deck towards the prow, holding down my damp dress as a gust of wind whips across the ship. Matteo stands perfectly still, his thin frame unaffected by the ship tilting again in the relentless wind. Maybe those big ears balance him!

He doesn't answer me, but instead takes the telescope that hangs around his neck on a piece of ragged leather and presses it against his left eye, scanning the horizon. Left to right and back again, over and over.

'Are you looking for pirates, Matteo?' I ask, standing next to him and following his gaze. A vast expanse of dense silvery-grey water gathers in angry white peaks that blend into the dark sky. The sun is all but hidden, although every now and then it interrupts the dome of moody sky with a flash of brightness.

'Pirates?' he asks casually, the telescope still glued to his eye socket. I am sure I detect a note of panic in his voice, but he is hiding it very well. 'Best you don't talk of pirates on this ship. Just as well we sailed into the waves straight on or we would have gone down in that storm. If a tall wave hits the ship side on, we're in serious trouble.'

'That sounds scary. Anyway, Dr Hamilton said something about being plundered.'

Matteo lets the telescope fall back down to his chest and looks at me. His left eye has a faint ring around it, as though he's wearing a monocle. 'I couldn't possibly comment.'

'But . . .' I lick my dry, salty lips. My hair is still damp with sea spray, my skin sticky. My tummy rumbles and I decide to change tack. 'Thank you for the bread last night. Is there any more food?'

'Nico! We just survived a serious storm and you're asking about food. I don't want to be mean, but this isn't an adventure for me. Sailing through storms is a matter of . . . well, life and death. There is a scarcity of food on this ship – we only eat the bread and biscuits that I bake and the fish that Etienne catches. And, in an emergency, dried meat. We have to be really careful not to get scurvy – which could mean losing our teeth.'

'I didn't expect . . .' I say, feeling stupid and small and horribly aware that while I might have read a lot, I have experienced very little of life.

'What *did* you expect, Nico?' Matteo leans back against the side of the ship. 'Did you think we'd be feasting on turtles from the West Indies that we keep in a tank in a special cabin? That we'd be digging into Italian sausages and French olives?'

'No!' I say, feeling the heat creep up my neck and into my cheeks. My eyes start to sting.

'You should just go to your cabin and sit out the end of the storm. If you are really hungry, eat some biscuits.'

I have always obeyed the *go-to-your-room* order, but I decide now is a good time to break that habit. I take a deep breath. 'Dr Hamilton says I should make myself useful. And I know there are only four people on the crew. I can be another pair of hands. Do you have any spare trousers?'

The seagulls shriek above us and a gust of wind sweeps across the deck, but Matteo still doesn't move. It's as though he is glued to the ship with invisible roots, his arms thin but sturdy branches.

'Fine,' he says finally, grabbing my arm before I topple backwards in the wind. 'Go to the captain's cabin. It's directly above the bread room. You can't miss it because it says "captain's cabin" on the door. There's a trunk in there with my initials on it. "M" for Matteo, "D" for D'Angelo. You can borrow the red trousers.'

'I can't wear red trousers! My brothers always wore red trousers!'

He sighs, releasing me. 'Then take the blue pair. I don't care. Take a jumper too, if you like.'

'But why is your trunk in the captain's cabin?' I ask.

'Because the captain is my father,' Matteo replies, flashing a smug grin. 'And he just saved your life by navigating the storm.'

6

The wind drops suddenly and I am able to open the door to the captain's cabin easily. My dress is still sodden, my legs still shaky. An iron stove in the corner sits atop a platform of bricks, presumably to stop it from overheating and setting fire to the wooden planks beneath. The stove is lit and the cabin feels like a warm hug.

I allow myself a loud sigh of relief as I look around. The cabin is almost twice the size of mine. There's a faded map of the world on one wall and, beneath it, a bookshelf, nailed to the floor and crammed with dog-eared books about sailing. There are two hammocks, one which appears to be piled with clothes.

'King! Is that you?' asks a deep voice, heavy with sleep.

Oh, not clothes. A person. This must be the captain!

'I'm not whoever King is,' I say, my voice a thin rasp.

'In which case you must be the accidental stowaway,' he says, his voice more irritated than curious. 'Let me take a look at you.'

A hand shoots out of the dark and grabs the lantern that was sitting atop the stove. The light blinds me. I stand up very straight and wipe my sodden hair away from my face.

The lantern moves and I can see him, lying on the hammock, one arm behind his head. He looks just like Matteo, long and lean, but with a huge black beard. His face is tanned and lined by the sun and, as his black hair is cut short, I can see that his ears stick out just like his son's.

'I only came here to get a pair of Matteo's trousers. Not the red ones. The blue ones. And maybe a spare jumper. I am freezing cold . . .'

'You will find it warmer by the stove.' His voice is slightly softer, but I'm not convinced he is happy to have been woken up by a strange girl with long black hair and a very straight fringe looking to borrow some clothes.

I stand with my head bowed, watching the water drip from my dress on to the smooth wooden floor as the heat slowly warms my back. I daren't look up in case he tells me to leave the cabin, to disembark the ship, to go home, even though it's not really home at all.

He doesn't speak and I can't bear the silence.

'Captain, may I look in Matteo's trunk? I can then leave you to rest.'

'Matteo told me that you were an accidental stowaway and Dr Hamilton then confirmed that you are a family friend. But why are you really here?'

If I have to lie about Aunt to protect her, then everything else I say must be sort-of-true. 'I came to see if *Anthos* was in the harbour. Dr Hamilton is famous and I had always longed to see his ship. I had no intention of coming on board. But then I followed a kitten on to the ship and fell asleep in the rowing boat.'

'A genuine stowaway, then.' The captain is still staring at the ceiling, but I am sure I see a smile forming. 'And Dr Hamilton doesn't mind you being here on *Anthos*? I only saw him briefly. It's not always clear what he thinks about anything not directly related to work . . .'

'He says that I can stay for a few days, so long as I make myself useful.'

'What do you know about sailing?'

'I know that you have to sail into waves head-on or there will be trouble.'

The captain laughs.

'You are an unusual child. What did you say your name was?'

'I didn't. It's Nico Cloud, sir.'

'Well, that really was some storm. Being a captain is very demanding in such big storms so I had to come and lie down afterwards. I do hope you have found your sea legs, Nico Cloud. Not everyone appreciates life at sea, it has to be said. I could tell you many stories about sailors who never stopped being sick at sea.'

'I am learning. I haven't been sick but my legs are still a bit wobbly.'

'Wobbly legs are to be expected in the first week. Perhaps you will be good company for Matteo, who has spent his entire life at sea and knows very little of girls or *terra firma*.' When he sees my blank face, he adds, 'It's a Latin term that literally means "firm ground". But in this instance it really means dry land. As I was saying, it would be good for Matteo to spend time with a *ragazza* – Italian for "girl".'

'Are you Italian?'

'Yes, from Sicily,' he says, sitting up and swinging his legs out of the hammock. He is dressed in smart navy trousers and a navy jacket, with a white shirt beneath. 'Anyway, we waited to set sail until now to avoid storms, but the weather this spring is so strange and unpredictable – it doesn't bode well. Luckily this room used to be the kitchen, so at least Matteo and I have a large stove to keep us warm. Where are you sleeping?'

'In the cabin next door, sir.'

'You don't have to call me "sir", Nico. "Captain" is fine.'

'Thank you, captain.'

He nods, grabs a waterproof jacket from a rusty coat hook and allows the wind to slam the door behind him.

*

With the captain gone, the cabin feels big and empty, as though his presence filled it up. I take the lantern and see that Matteo's trunk is tucked in beneath his hammock. It takes a huge effort to pull it out, but Matteo must use it all the time because there's not a single speck of dust on its smooth wooden lid. I trace his initials with my fingertip and carefully undo the leather straps. The trunk is lined with pale blue cotton that is badly ripped, but the contents are beautifully arranged. On the left is a perfectly-folded pile of shirts and jumpers, in the middle are three pairs of trousers and on the right a few keepsakes.

My hand hovers over the right-hand pile. These are probably Matteo's most treasured possessions: three books of poetry, a round painting no bigger than a dinner plate and a hand-sewn toy with large, floppy ears that looks like a rabbit – no, a hare. I glance at the door. I can risk looking, if I am quick. I want to know him better.

Maybe we can even be friends. His father said I could be good for him, after all.

I carefully take the round painting out of the trunk and hold it up to the light of the fire. The paint has slightly faded with time, but it's still exquisite, the strokes of the brush delicate and the woman's face luminous. She must have been staring straight at the artist. Her blue eyes are serious but her mouth is playfully turned up at the edges. There's a dimple on her left cheek. Her dark, lustrous hair is tied in a neat bun. I decide immediately that I would have liked her. She is so very young, surely not much older than nineteen. Who is she?

'Nico? Put that back!'

The painting drops out of my hands, back into the trunk. I freeze. Even though my back is turned to Matteo, I can feel his surprise and fury. I daren't even turn round.

Neither of us speak. The air becomes heavy, like the thickest fog. I wonder if Matteo has his hands on his hips, elbows jutting out. I force myself to stand up and face him.

'I am truly sorry,' I say, stepping towards him. 'I was looking for your trousers and . . . I didn't hear you come in.'

He just looks at me.

'Say something, Matteo.' Silence. 'Who is the woman

in the painting?'

He thrusts both his hands into his trouser pockets.

I carry on. 'I like the look of her. She's very striking.'

He smiles and I see the dimple in his left cheek for the first time.

'Is she your sister?' I ask. 'Where does she live?'

He shakes his head. 'She's not my sister. And she's dead.'

The words sound final, as though that's the end of the conversation.

'I'm very sorry for your loss,' I say, as gently as I can.

He shrugs. 'She died fourteen years ago.'

I think for a moment. 'Didn't you say you are fourteen?'

'Yes.' He swallows. 'It was my fault. She died in childbirth.'

Goosebumps race down my arms and legs. 'Your mother,' I whisper. I want to ask a hundred questions.

Instead, I hold my arms out. I don't know how to hug, but I think this might be a good start. He lifts his head and swiftly wipes the tears away with the back of his hand and then wipes his hand on his trousers.

'Please don't feel sorry for me,' he says. And then he starts talking fast, filling the room with words, as though he doesn't want to risk me asking any more questions. 'You need to change out of your wet clothes before you catch a chill. Take whichever trousers you prefer, a shirt and a jumper. There's a spare raincoat on the back of the door. It was mine until I grew out of it. You can have it. I will wait for you outside.' He pauses. 'I'm sorry that I snapped at you earlier. Big storms are very demanding.' I smile to myself; he sounds just like his father. 'Don't take long, we have work to do.'

He said 'we'! I nod and he closes the door behind him.

As I change, I notice that although his clothes are clean, they still smell of seaweed and salt and fish and smoke.

When I leave the cabin and step outside, the sky is bright blue, the air fresh, the sea calm. I allow myself to exhale deeply. The storm has passed.

Matteo laughs when he sees me in his clothes and I suddenly feel self-conscious in the turned-up blue trousers and red woollen jumper, my black hair tied up with some string I found in the chest.

He shoves me playfully as I approach. 'That's better. I've yet to see a sailor in a dress.'

I smile. 'Hardly surprising since women have been forbidden aboard ships since 1808.'

'Poppycock,' says Matteo.

'What do you mean?'

'Oh. You know – hogwash.'

'I know what the *word* means, I was asking what *you* mean? Do you think women should be forced to stay on *terra firma*?'

He pauses for a moment and I can almost see the thoughts whirring through his head. 'My mother gave birth to me on a ship,' he says at last, 'so I say poppycock to the rules.'

'Were you born on *this* ship?'

He looks away, towards the three billowing sails, each the shape of an enormous seagull wing.

'You wanted to learn about sailing,' he says. 'A ship has three or more masts and is longer than 197 feet. Or, to put it more simply, a boat can fit on a ship but a ship cannot fit on a boat. *Anthos* is a small ship, but she's definitely a ship.'

'I have a question. If the ship is a *she*, why aren't women allowed on board?'

'Good question,' says Matteo. 'But I don't make the rules. Anyway, a ship is divided crossways into three parts: the fore, the midship and the aft.'

'Which part are we standing on?' I desperately want Matteo to give me a proper tour but I know I must be patient.

'We're standing in the midship.' I feel silly – that was obvious, we're in the middle – but Matteo doesn't seem to mind.

'The sail at the front of the boat is the foremast. The one in the middle, the biggest one, is the mainmast and the smaller one at the end is the mizzenmast.' He guides me to the side of the ship so we have a better view. 'You see that man up there at the top of the mainsail? That's Claude. I'll introduce you later.'

I peer up at Claude, whose sun-bleached hair seems

to have a life of its own, sticking up at strange angles as though it's never seen a comb. He seems to be completely comfortable up there, at the top of the mainsail. His white shirt billows in the wind as though it's a separate sail – he doesn't seem to be bothered by the fact that a strong gust of wind could blow him away.

'Nico? Are you listening? See those small sails at the front? They're the jibs. The helm of the ship is where you'll find the ship's wheel, used to steer along with the rudder and the tiller. The stern is the aftermost end of the ship. The keep is the lowest part of the ship. And when we say "galley", we mean kitchen.'

Matteo stops and smiles at a boy who is swabbing the deck. The boy appears to be a similar age to Matteo and is almost as wide as he is tall – it is the boy who not so long ago was frantically battening down the hatches.

'Oh, hello, Etienne,' Matteo says.

Etienne's blond hair is cut short and he is wearing a

white T-shirt and navy trousers turned up at the bottom.

'Etienne Levi, meet Nico Cloud. Nico, Etienne. He's Claude's son.'

Etienne reaches out a rough, calloused hand and he shakes mine so firmly that I fear he will break at least one of the twenty-seven bones in my hand.

'I saw you during the storm I think. Nice to meet you properly, Nico Cloud,' he says, with a soft French accent. 'Are you a friend of Matteo's?'

'We've only just met,' Matteo replies. I stare at the deck, feeling oddly disappointed.

There is an awkward silence and I realise Etienne is waiting to be told who I am and what I am doing on *Anthos*.

'Dr Hamilton is a family friend,' I say. 'He gave me permission to stay on the ship for a few days.'

Etienne cocks his head and leans against the side of the ship, arms crossed. 'The thing is . . .'

'I'm a girl? I know.'

'I mean . . .' He looks nervously at Matteo. 'We don't want to get in trouble for hiding you.'

'Don't worry, Etienne. Nico will disembark when we drop anchor at Cuckmere Haven in the next day or two.'

I wish they would all stop saying that!

'Very well,' says Etienne, pulling at a thread hanging from his shirt. There's another awkward pause.

'Who is King?' I ask, to change the subject. 'The captain mentioned him.'

Etienne freezes. Matteo's cheeks colour. They shake their heads at each other.

They can have as many secrets as they like, I think. Neither has a clue about the true identity of Dr Hamilton.

'I don't believe that Father mentioned Mr King to you,' says Matteo, his face like thunder.

'I think he was talking in his sleep,' I say.

'He was?' Matteo sounds surprised – and disappointed.

'That's almost as bad! Look. We can't talk here. Come with us to the sick bay.'

*

We march to the prow of the ship, climb down some steps and enter a small room. The air in the sick bay is stale, with a distant smell of disinfectant. It is spotlessly clean. There are five hammocks strung between the walls, each with a beige blanket folded neatly in the middle. Matteo and Etienne sit side by side on an old, scratched wooden table and I stand in front of them, my hands behind my back, as though I'm on trial.

Embarrassed, I try to sit on the edge of a hammock, my legs dangling beneath me, and wobble all over the place.

'Hammocks are for lying on, not sitting on,' says Matteo.

'Sit on the steps?' suggests Etienne.

I do. The wood beneath me is cold, but I try to sit still.

The boys, sitting shoulder to shoulder, chew on their lips.

Matteo takes a deep breath. There is no sign of his dimple. 'If we tell you about Mr King, you must promise not to tell *anyone*. Not your parents, assuming they are alive. Not your brothers who wear red trousers. Not your friends, assuming you have any.'

'I promise on Astra's life,' I say. 'My kitten,' I add, when Etienne looks confused.

'Very well,' says Matteo. 'Herman King is a ruthless man who is only interested in money. He has a son called Otis to whom he apparently shows little love or kindness. We haven't met them, but even Father, who generally thinks the best of people, believes that King is wicked.'

'He sounds horrible,' I say. My bum is getting numb. 'But I still don't understand why everyone is being so *weird* about him. What's the fuss all about?'

Matteo and Etienne exchange glances. Etienne

shrugs and pulls a piece of paper and a pencil out of his pocket. He sits there expectantly, as though he is about to take notes.

'The "fuss" is that Dr Hamilton is doing some very important research,' says Matteo.

I knew it! Those empty vials and the soil had told me that. 'What kind of research?' I ask.

Matteo shrugs. 'Dr Hamilton's study door is nearly always locked and the doctor is very rarely seen – at meal times, we generally knock three times and then leave food outside the door. So none of us really knows what goes on down there. But Father tells me that the doctor might have discovered something that will end up changing the world.' He pauses. 'Mr King has been employed by a group of scientists who work at a university in London. If he can steal Dr Hamilton's work and take it to them, then they will pay him a lot of money.'

'Are those scientists all men?' I ask.

'Of course,' says Matteo. 'Why do you ask?'

I stand up and walk across the room, which is only seven steps wide, so I have to turn back almost immediately. 'That's unfair,' I say.

It's chilly in the sick bay and I hug my arms around me, grateful for Matteo's heavy woollen jumper. 'I'm as curious about the world as any boy, but when I'm older I'm supposed to stay at home and cook for my husband.'

'That's ridiculous,' says Etienne, chewing the end of his pencil.

'Neither of us knew our mothers,' says Matteo. 'And there are only men on board *Anthos*. We know that women aren't allowed on ships, which everyone in this sick bay agrees is ridiculous. But we don't know much more about women than that.'

I wish I could tell them the truth about Aunt. But I can't. So, instead, I tell them about one of my favourite scientists.

'Well,' I say. 'I once read about a German scientist and artist called Maria Sibylla Merian who was born in 1647. Her passion was entomology – the study of insects. Insects were often seen as the beasts of the devil, but she didn't care. She was really interested in silkworms and caterpillars and learned how to draw them as a child, recording each stage of their life cycles. She was even allowed to bring a colony of silkworms into her home to study. Can you imagine being allowed to do that?'

Etienne swings his feet back and forth, faster and faster, until Matteo elbows him in the ribs.

'I *am* listening,' says Etienne. But he doesn't appear to be; his pencil is busy gliding across the paper.

'Anyway,' I continue, 'a famous naturalist was convinced he'd worked out how butterflies are made. He thought that butterflies lived inside caterpillars' bodies. He said he could prove that his theory was true by doing something with boiling water, vinegar and wine. What an odd man. But Maria knew that couldn't be true. She had worked out that butterflies have a continuous life cycle. When she was thirty-two, Maria published two books that showed how metamorphosis works. She proved that the caterpillar goes through several stages: egg to larva to chrysalis to butterfly. Or, of course, moth.'

'Like this?' asks Etienne, showing me a beautiful drawing of a caterpillar shrugging off its chrysalis.

'Exactly like that!' I say. 'That's amazing, Etienne.'

Etienne's cheeks colour and he swings his legs even faster.

Matteo seems to be thinking hard. At last, he says, 'Do you think Dr Hamilton is working on something as amazing as Maria Sibylla Merian?'

'I don't know,' I say. 'But we have to protect Dr Hamilton's work at all costs. We must defend him against Mr King and his son!'

'Pirate King, you mean,' mutters Etienne.

'Pirate Herman and Pirate Boy Otis!' I say, more loudly than I intended and put my arms up as if ready for battle.

Etienne giggles, but Matteo looks serious. 'Don't let Dr Hamilton hear you call them pirates,' he says. 'He's a stickler for precision and that includes people's titles.'

'Oh come on,' I say. 'He will never find out.'

'Go on, Matteo,' Etienne says. 'Say it!'

Matteo leaps off the table. 'Fine. We will protect Dr Hamilton and *Anthos* against Pirate King and Pirate Boy Otis.'

Etienne and I burst out laughing and Matteo can't stop himself from joining in. I forget to feel anxious, forget that I have only just met these boys, forget that my time on the ship might soon be over. It feels so good to laugh and be silly. I had forgotten how the warm glow of happiness feels.

'Come on,' says Matteo, pulling Etienne off the table. 'Let's show Nico Cloud what a real sunset looks like.'

7

We emerge from the sick bay moments later to find that *Anthos* is drifting through gentle waves, her sails fluttering in the breeze. Etienne carefully fixes two fishing rods made of dark wood to the side of the ship.

'You never know, we might catch a fish or two for supper,' he says, to himself as much as anyone else.

I stand next to Matteo at the bow of the ship.

'What do you think?' he asks, nodding at the horizon.

At home, the sunset would sometimes momentarily colour my bedroom the intense red of a blushing cheek, but this is something else. As the gulls swoop expectantly around Etienne's fishing rods, the sun slowly but surely slips out of sight, a vast sphere of bright orange casting a golden reflection on to the iron-grey sea. The sky is pink and red and orange all at once, the wispy black clouds the only reminder of the brutal storm earlier.

'I've never seen a sunset like this,' I say.

We stand in comfortable silence, leaning against the side of the ship, looking out to sea.

'I can't wait to see the moon!' I exclaim, disturbing the peaceful moment. 'I was watching it out of my bedroom window two nights ago, before I was told to go to sleep or else go without food the next day. It was waxing then, I think. Perhaps we shall see a full moon before I have to leave the ship.'

'Your mother and father sound . . . a little cruel,' says Matteo carefully, as though he doesn't want to say the wrong thing. 'Is that why you ran away?'

'I didn't really mean to run away . . . but yes, they can be cruel. They are certainly strict. And old-fashioned. It's not like we live in the 1700s, for goodness' sake. They are confused because I love science and girls aren't meant to. My younger twin brothers are not remotely interested in books. They are eight and all they want to do is roll around and play.'

'That's pretty much what most children do at that age, I'm afraid,' says Matteo. 'Anyway, I am sure your parents will be missing you.'

'I doubt it,' I say, quickly. 'At least you and Etienne have fathers who want to spend time with you.'

'At least you have a mother *and* a father,' he says, his voice suddenly as spiky as a sea urchin. 'I barely met my mother. And Etienne never talks about this, but his mother was swept overboard in a storm just before his third birthday. He might not say much, but all his feelings come out in his drawings.'

A wave of panic washes over me. How foolish of me to try and compare our lives, to make him and Etienne out to be the lucky ones.

'I'm sorry,' I say eventually, forcing those difficult words out of my mouth without any hint of sulkiness. 'Sometimes when I don't know what to say the words come out all wrong. I'm glad you told me about your mother. I'm sorry about Etienne's too.'

The air carries a chill, the sky is deep blue, the sea an

inky black and the stars are starting to wink at us.

'Is that your tummy rumbling again?' asks Matteo. I nod, embarrassed, but this time he is smiling. 'Let's eat. It looks like Etienne has prepared a feast.'

We must have been chatting and looking out at the horizon for a long time, because when I turn around, I see that Etienne has built a fire in a steel bowl balanced on two parallel wooden planks. Three fish are skewered on a branch that's been stripped of its leaves, their scales burning ever darker as Etienne slowly turns them to ensure they are cooked evenly. A pot of soup in a corner of the fire bubbles gently and a plate of freshly baked bread sits in a bowl, torn into chunks of pieces. *A proper feast!*

'Don't get ideas,' says Matteo, as we sit down and join Etienne. 'It won't always be like this, but we wanted to welcome you properly.'

'Thank you, Etienne! And Matteo, of course.'

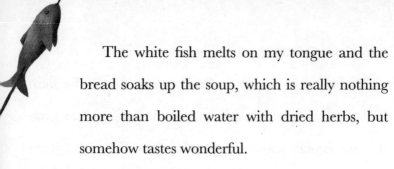

The white fish melts on my tongue and the bread soaks up the soup, which is really nothing more than boiled water with dried herbs, but somehow tastes wonderful.

Etienne pulls the last fragments of flesh off the fish bones with his teeth and Matteo mops up the dregs of the soup from the pan.

'Where's the captain – and Claude?' I ask, wiping my mouth on my sleeve because there don't seem to be any napkins.

'You really were hungry,' Matteo says, laughing. 'Claude is having his supper in his room and the captain will be joining us shortly. Etienne took Dr Hamilton his food while you and I were talking.'

'Who sails the ship at night?' I ask.

'We take it in turns to sail and keep watch,' says Etienne. 'Around midnight, all being well, we will drop anchor near Cuckmere Haven. And then it's Matteo's turn to keep watch till dawn.'

My heart sinks. If we are so close to land again, Etienne will be able to row me to shore and leave me on the beach and that will be that. My adventure will be over. I will have no idea how to get home and if I ever do make it, I'll be sent to my room for ever. And if I try to explain *why* I left in the first place, Mother will doubtless tell me that no one wants to hear my voice and then the twins will mimic her for days – 'No one wants to hear you, Nico, no one no one no one no one!' – before dissolving into fits of giggles.

What can I offer Matteo and Etienne, to persuade them to let me stay? Or, for that matter, Aunt Ruth? I barely know which side of the ship is port and which is starboard. I don't know how to navigate, I can't mend sails, I can't fish, I can barely even cook.

'You look as white as a ghost, Nico,' says Matteo. 'What are you thinking about?'

'Oh, nothing,' I say, forcing a smile. It's easier to turn the attention away from me and be the one who is asking the questions. 'What will you do in Cuckmere Haven?'

'Dr Hamilton is interested in the fossils there,' says Matteo.

'The chalk is a soft white limestone made up of the skeletons of tiny marine plants,' I say. 'I imagine you can find ammonites, sea urchins . . .'

'I'm sure you can,' says Matteo. 'I will be looking for fossils, as instructed by Dr Hamilton, and Etienne will forage for some food. We're on a six-month voyage around the British Isles with pretty much only rat-infested sacks of flour to keep us going. We can't very well live on bread and fish.'

I could spare some of my seeds, I think suddenly. The ones that grow fast, like radishes, salad leaves and red peppers. Aunt has that box of soil in her cabin, hidden under the cloth. She can surely spare a little. There is a large bucket in the shade of the middle sail – the mainsail – collecting rainwater. There should be plenty of sun. Within four weeks they'd have something healthy to eat. I clench and unclench my fists. I don't want to beg. At the same time, I don't want to leave. If Matteo is fossil hunting, I want to go too. If Aunt is inventing something life changing, I want to help her.

'Perhaps . . .' I say hesitantly.

The boys look at me.

'Go on, Nico,' says Matteo. 'Tell us. What have you got to lose?'

I stare at the fire and bite my nails. I couldn't bear it if they laughed at my passion for seeds in the same way Father used to laugh at me. So I say nothing.

Matteo shrugs. 'We can drop you off in Cuckmere Haven tomorrow. Walk from the shore towards the road and I imagine you will find a mail coach willing to give you a lift back towards Emsworth if you explain that you are lost.'

I look at Etienne, but he is busy drawing a picture of the fish bone on his plate.

'Good evening, *ragazzi*,' says the captain, who seems to have appeared out of nowhere. 'Claude is still busy mending the sails that were ripped in the storm, so don't forget to save him some food.'

'"*Ragazzi*" means "kids" or "you lot",' Matteo explains to me. 'Sit down here, Papà! We saved you some fish and bread and soup. Will you tell us one of your folklore stories? I'm sure Nico would love to hear it.'

'Do you believe in folklore, captain?' I ask, thinking about how I adored *The Book of Lore and Legends*.

'Why not? I grew up in Sicily with stories that my *bisnonna*, my great-grandmother, used to tell my *nonna*, my grandmother. Why do you ask, Nico?'

'When I was younger,' I say, 'I read about a mythical Sicilian tree from a long, long time ago that was surrounded by olive trees and bore jewel-like fruit even in the winter.' I take my notebook out of my pocket and tentatively show him my childish drawing.

The captain smiles. 'Ah, *l'Albero della Speranza*. The Tree of Hope.'

Goosebumps travel up my arms and down my legs.

The captain grins. 'According to my *nonna*, a greedy bird who was too fat to fly gobbled up all the seeds,' he says, smoothing his beard as he talks. 'The locals were rarely, if ever, brave enough to go near the tree even when they were starving and the fruit looked delicious. Obviously my *nonna* never saw the tree – her mother, my *bisnonna* simply told her about it – but she seemed to truly believe that it had once existed.'

The captain knows about the Tree of Hope! Which means . . . maybe, just maybe, it did exist at some point. I want to say something, but I just sit there, my jaw hanging open.

I look at Matteo, who is equally entranced. 'Do *you*

think the tree exists, Papà?' he asks.

'I really don't know, *amore*,' replies the captain, pausing to nibble the remaining fish from the bone. 'As you know, myths are traditional stories that help to explain where we came from and who we are – you could say that Sicily is an island built on myths.'

Matteo takes the captain's hand in his. 'Papà, tell us the Sicilian myth of the ghost ship? I'm pretty sure Nico won't have heard it!'

The captain kisses Matteo's hand and my heart aches unexpectedly; my father never showed me such tenderness.

'It's a simple story, really,' he says, looking at me. 'Santa Lucia is a martyr who lived in Sicily at the

start of the fourth century. She was best known for two things: performing incredible miracles, and the food associated with her. Santa Lucia was often shown in medieval paintings carrying a dish that contained her eyes; she is known as the patron saint of sight. She was condemned to death by fire for her religious beliefs, but it didn't work – she was killed with a sword in the end.'

Etienne puts a hand to his neck, as though feeling for a wound. I ask him if I can borrow his pencil, open my notebook and try to draw Santa Lucia carrying a dish with her own eyes on it.

'What has Santa Lucia got to do with the ghost ship?' I ask, as I sketch.

'I'm coming to that. Santa Lucia's feast day falls on 13th December. To celebrate, Sicilians often eat *panelle* – chickpea fritters – and a pudding known as *cuccìa*, made from boiled wheat grain.' He pronounces the word slowly. *Coo-cchee-a*. 'They eat such things because there was a famine in Palermo, the capital of Sicily, in the middle of the seventeenth century. Much of the population was starving after a catastrophic wheat harvest left them without any bread . . .'

'No bread,' Matteo says, and pulls a face.

The captain smiles. 'You can imagine, *tesoro*, how desperate they were. I know we're always saying we're hungry here on *Anthos*, but we have no idea what it's like not to know when the next plate of food might appear.'

'The ghost ship, Papà!'

'You are so impatient, son. I am getting to it now. The people of Palermo prayed for help. And then, on 13th December 1646 – just over 150 years ago – a miracle happened. A ship packed full of wheat arrived in the port in Palermo. No one knew who had sent the ship; it was empty. As if it was run by ghosts. People stormed the ship and started to eat the raw wheat. They were so hungry that they didn't even bother to mill it into flour, to make bread.'

I sketch a ship full of people, looking as hungry as the girl in the doorway at Emsworth. I draw cats in the shape of loaves.

'Did the people of Palermo think that Santa Lucia sent the ship?' asks Etienne. He takes a spare pencil from behind his ear and taps it on his knee.

The captain nods. 'They did. And still today, on 13th December, Sicilians celebrate Santa Lucia's feast day by eating *cuccìa*. Sometimes plain boiled grain, perhaps with some olive oil and cinnamon, or, if they are lucky, with sweetened ricotta.'

'I would love to go to Sicily and learn about more myths,' I say. 'Can you imagine if the Tree of Hope really existed? If it did, then there might well be fossilised seeds that could somehow create another tree . . .'

'Now you're just getting carried away,' says Matteo, laughing.

'Well . . .' says the captain, smoothing down his beard again. 'Maybe she's not. Nonna once took me to the botanical garden in Palermo. She said there was a small dark room in a building on the other side of the hot house where fossilised Tree of Hope seeds were kept. We went inside but we couldn't find anything. There *was* a room, but it was locked and it looked as though no one had been inside it for a very long time.'

I draw a sign at the top of the page saying, 'PALERMO' and, just below it, 'BOTANICAL GARDEN'. I sketch a greenhouse full of exotic plants and an arrow leading to a small room with a key in the door. I write 'TREE OF HOPE?' next to the room. I can almost taste the dust in the locked room. It's just a story, but I want it so badly to be true. I know scientists are supposed to believe facts and not fiction, but I can't help believing they might complement one another.

The captain stands up and brushes breadcrumbs off

his navy blue trousers. 'Now it's time for bed. It's been a long day,  with an unexpected storm, and we have a busy day tomorrow.'

I stand up without wobbling. Maybe I am getting my sea legs after all. Even better, for the first time all day, I don't feel sick.

'Good night, everyone,' I say. I look up at the stars above us, shining more brightly than I have ever seen them. I can't believe this is my last day on the ship. I can't bear to think about what will happen when I am sent home to Mother and Father.

'Good night, Nico,' they say in unison, their voices carefree, as though the world is still a good place. 'Sweet dreams.'

I trudge back to my cabin and am surprised to see that a fire has been lit while we were having supper. I must remember to thank Claude – I can't imagine it was Aunt Ruth. Astra is lying on her back in front of the fire, all four feet poking straight up into the air. It's tempting to rub my face in her white belly fur and kiss the soft pink pads on her paws, but we barely know one another.

Instead I sit down next her, my chin on my knees, and offer her the pieces of fish left over from supper. She gulps the food down and wraps herself around my legs, offering me love in return.

8

9 April 1832

The woman with the white dress and hands full of golden light is drifting in a tranquil sea. She is walking through a glass room of green leaves and orange and red flowers. She is on her knees, her cupped hands offering the golden light. She is beneath the water, trying to talk. I listen but I can't hear any words. Someone is here, in my cabin, taking Astra away—

'Nico! Nico! Wake up! I need your help!'

Matteo's hot breath is on my face.

He is clutching Astra to his chest.

I sit up, swing my legs to the side and push myself out

of the hammock, which I do easily – not because I am now such an experienced sailor, but because it's not moving at all. In fact, it is perfectly still.

'What is it?' I ask, rubbing my eyes. I've always been rubbish in the morning and I'm extra rubbish after a weird dream. I remember a woman in my cabin, with golden light in her hands. Ridiculous.

'Come with me,' says Matteo, putting Astra down gently in front of the stove.

'Are you making me leave already?' I ask.

Matteo doesn't answer; he simply pushes me outside on to the deck. He leans over the bow of the ship, so far, in fact, that he looks as though he might flip over into the sea. The fog is so dense that I can barely see his ears.

'Matteo!' I say, shouting over the wind. 'What's going on?'

'We dropped anchor and it was my turn to keep watch. I saw a boy in a boat rowing towards *Anthos* . . .'

I look around. 'Where's Etienne?'

Matteo points in the direction of the sea. 'We lowered the rowing boat – the one you fell asleep in – into the sea so he could take a closer look.'

'On his own?'

Matteo swallows. 'Yes. And now I can't see him. Nor the boy. I woke you up as a last resort.'

As a last resort! Thanks a lot, I think.

'What about the captain and Claude?'

'I haven't woken them. They will be furious if they find out Etienne went off on his own.'

'I can see why.' I think for a moment. 'Is there another boat we could use?'

Matteo shakes his head. 'No. I'm sorry I woke you. I just . . .'

'You did the right thing. Let's walk around the edges of the ship together and see if we can see anything as we wait for the fog to lift.'

'Good idea,' says Matteo. 'But we can't shout Etienne's name because Father and Claude will wake up. Or, worse, Dr Hamilton might hear us.'

'Right,' I say.

If Etienne's life might be at risk, is it better to be shouted at for trying to save him or to be shouted at for not managing to save him? I keep my thoughts to myself.

We walk from the prow to the stern, down the starboard side and back along the port side, staring into the steady gloom. The fog is like a grey wall, concealing us from the rest of the world.

'Stop,' whispers Matteo. 'Did you hear that?'

I strain my ears.

A seagull screeches overhead. I can hear a faint noise. Then the prow of a rowing boat pokes its nose through the fog in the water below.

Matteo rummages frantically around in a large box and pulls out a long rope ladder. He drops it over the side of the ship and quickly ties it to the rails with two complicated-looking knots.

'Don't, Matteo. It's too big a risk. Please.'

He pulls the knots tight.

'The water will be too cold. Matteo. Please.'

He slips off his boots, drops his coat to the floor and swings one long leg over the side of the ship. And then the other.

I look at the captain's cabin, willing Matteo's father to appear.

Matteo is already halfway down the ladder.

Matteo, holding the ladder so tightly that his knuckles are white, turns his head. Waves rise up and splash the hull of the ship. His socks are splattered with salty water.

'Etienne?' Matteo's voice is barely above a whisper.

The rowing boat pushes closer. The tips of the wooden oars appear. And then Etienne's battered brown leather boots, at the end of his stretched-out legs.

'Thank goodness,' I say to myself.

'What are you doing?' Etienne asks, peering up at Matteo.

'Looking for you,' says Matteo, pulling himself back up the ladder. 'It was stupid to let you go off unaccompanied into the fog looking for a strange boy.'

'Well, I couldn't see anything,' says Etienne.

Etienne stands at the front of the rowing boat – I would have wobbled and fallen in, no question – and checks that the long piece of rope attached to its bow is secure. He takes a step back and throws the remaining rope up at Matteo, who catches it first time. Matteo swiftly ties a sailor's knot on the ship's railing and waits for Etienne to climb the ladder.

Matteo pulls his boots back on over his wet socks and puts a hand on Etienne's shoulder when he makes it to the deck. 'Glad you're back safely. Best not to mention any of this to the captain or Claude.'

Etienne nods. 'Whatever you think.'

'Are you leaving the rowing boat there?' I ask, looking down at the water.

'Yes,' says Matteo. 'Till the fog clears and we are all ready to disembark.'

And, in my case, go home.

We stand on the deck in silence, and suddenly it's warm and the sun is shining, and it's as though the fog was never there. We are closer to the coast than I realised;

the fog obscured the view. And what a view. The tide is in and the narrow strip of pebble beach looks like a good spot for a picnic. Out here, the sea is a dark bluey-grey, but closer to shore it is a pale, greeny-blue. Maybe it's the chalk in the soil that lightens it.

'There's some bread for breakfast,' says Matteo.

'Great,' I say, tearing my eyes away from the view. 'By the way,' I say as casually as I can, ' did the boy on the rowing boat have lots of dark, curly hair?'

'He did. Really wild curls like Father has if he doesn't bother cutting it for a while.' Matteo frowns. 'Why do you ask?'

I think I might just be starting to piece the mystery together. Matteo and Etienne talked about Otis King, whose father is desperate to steal my aunt's work. And now a boy, who sounds very much like the boy I met at the port, appears out of nowhere. It's suspicious, but I don't want to alert them to what might be a coincidence just yet.

'No reason,' I say, looking away.

'I'm starving,' says Etienne, already heading towards the galley. We follow, our tummies rumbling in unison.

*

'Can I see your drawings from last night?' asks Etienne, sitting forward on the galley bench, his mouth full of bread.

'I'm not nearly as good as you,' I say.

He shrugs. 'It doesn't matter. I'm just curious.' Matteo nods, as if he too is curious.

'OK,' I say, rather pleased at their interest. 'I'll go and get my notebook from my cabin now.'

*

The notebook is not in my hammock. I try to remember where I put it when I returned to the cabin after dinner last night. The pencil is still in my left pocket. I rummage through my bag. Not there. I empty the contents – the seeds, the map of Europe, the spare dress, a corner of newspaper – out on to the floor. It's *definitely* not there. I start to feel sick.

I open the stove door to see if my notebook ended up in there. No sign of it. I lift Astra up in case she's sitting on it. She's not. A feeling of dread creeps up my spine. Fragments of my dream start to reappear. What if it wasn't a dream; what if someone was in my room. What if it wasn't a woman with gold light in her hands, but the pirate boy!

I think furiously. He must have boarded *Anthos* under the cover of the fog, snuck into my room and stolen the notebook. What would he want with it? Inside is my drawing of the Tree of Hope, a map of the botanical garden and the arrows to the locked room where the captain's *nonna* thought the fossilised seeds might be kept. But that's just a story. Isn't it?

Unless . . . Maybe the boys are playing games with me. That's the real reason they asked to see my drawings. I dash out of the cabin and across the deck and into the galley, where Etienne is still pulling at pieces of bread and Matteo is washing the dishes in a bucket of seawater.

'I can't find my notebook. Is it here?'

Etienne shakes his head.

'Give it back!' I yell, surprised at the force of my voice.

'What's going on, Nico?' Matteo asks, putting a gentle hand on my shoulder.

My heart is hammering. I shrug his hand away. 'If you don't have it, the boy on the boat must have stolen it.'

Matteo frowns. 'Calm down, Nico.'

'We don't have it. I promise,' Etienne says, popping the last piece of bread in his mouth. I look at them both and I can see they are not lying.

There is only one thing for it. I need to speak to my aunt.

Aunt Ruth's door is, as always, closed. I knock, tentatively at first and then more firmly. There's a small round hole in the door at about face height that I haven't noticed before and I'm sure there's a deep grey eye on the other side, but when I put my own eye to the hole, there's only blackness.

'Dr Hamilton? It's me, Nico. It's urgent.'

Finally, a key turns the middle lock and then a second at the top of the door and a third at the bottom. The enhanced security must be there to prevent the Kings from entering her study. I am glad she is so protected – especially since I am now pretty sure that the pirate boy was on *Anthos* only an hour or so ago.

Aunt doesn't open the door very wide, but I go in anyway.

'What is it, Nico?' she asks, walking back to her desk, her back to me.

I blurt it all out. 'A boy stole my notebook! He came aboard the ship in the fog and broke into my cabin and stole it.' Then I burst into tears.

'Slow down, child,' she says. 'Sit there, on the armchair.'

I hadn't noticed the armchair before. It must have been covered in books – perhaps she tidied up since my last visit. I sit down, my clammy legs sticking to the brown leather, and wipe my snotty face on my sleeve.

'A boy didn't take your notebook,' says Aunt, a slightly embarrassed smile creeping across her face. 'I did.'

She opens a drawer, lifts out my notebook and places it on her desk. I sigh the biggest ever sigh of relief.

She continues. 'I went to the galley at dawn to get some bread for breakfast. I saw the notebook on top of a pile of plates. I recognised it immediately as the one I gave you all those years ago. Anyway, I brought it back here for safekeeping. I don't believe anyone would be able to board the ship, by the way, not unless they found a way to throw a ladder up and over the side from a wobbly rowing boat. But if he had stolen your notebook, the map of the botanical garden in Palermo was quite the giveaway – that is, *if* we are to believe that the Tree of Hope existed and *if* its fossilised seeds are kept there. Anyway, here's your notebook. Keep it safe.'

I open it and my heart skips a beat. There, next to my pretty basic sketch of the botanical garden, is the most intricate and exquisite illustration of a fruit. It looks like an ancient pomegranate, with fruit bursting out of its tough skin. There is also a cross-section of fossilised seeds as though examined under a microscope. The seeds would doubtless just look like a dull collection of slightly irregular circles to most people, but to me they are as exciting as a dozen shooting stars collected in one place.

'Aunt . . . Did *you* draw this?' I ask.

She puts her hand over her heart and fiddles with something – Grandma's jet brooch. 'I got a little carried away,' she says. 'I hope you don't mind.'

My brain is whirring. 'Does that mean . . . do you believe the tree existed?'

'Now you are putting words into my mouth.' She

takes off her glasses and rubs her eyes with the heel of her hand. There are dark semi-circles beneath her eyes. Her shoulders are slumped. She looks exhausted.

'Aunt?'

She looks at me and smiles. 'Even scientists can dream, Nico.'

9

I can hear muffled voices outside and the sounds of boots running up and down the deck; we must be approaching land.

I look at my aunt. This might be the last time I see her. I can feel my bottom lip wobbling, but I'm determined not to cry. Finally, I get up from the armchair and stand as straight as a ruler in the middle of the cabin.

'I can hear the boys looking for me – they are ready to drop me off at Cuckmere Haven. I have to go now, Aunt. For ever. Thank you for having me. Goodbye.'

She holds her glasses up to the porthole to examine them for smudges.

'Unless . . . I can grow food for us all,' I blurt out.

Aunt looks confused.

'With my seeds! The radishes and red peppers would come up in no time and by summer we could have more tomatoes than we could possibly eat. The red peppers are full of vitamin C and would ward off ailments like scurvy. Matteo told me all about it.' She is silent, but at least she hasn't said no. *Keep going.* 'I could also help you with the fossil hunting. I have read so much about excavating fossils . . .'

I pause to draw breath. Aunt's eyes are narrowed.

She takes her pipe off the desk and lights it. I'm getting used to the smell. She turns to the side table adjacent to her desk and whips the cloth off, like a magician. Several of the vials are half-full of soil while the rest are empty. Next to a neat row of fossils are some brushes, a magnifying glass, a microscope and a pair of goggles.

'I don't know how close I am to fulfilling my life's work,' says Aunt.

'What is holding you back?' I ask.

'The simple answer? The right fossilised seed. The seed has to be intact. It has to be in *perfect* condition after thousands of years in a fossilised state. It's a big ask, Nico.'

'And once you find the right fossilised seed?'

'I am pretty sure I can place it in one of these

vials, alongside this special soil' – she indicates the box of damp earth – 'and bingo! The seed will grow, flower and create seeds of its own. If we could actually make it work, it will be a miracle.'

We! If we can make it work.

I try to assemble my thoughts. If she finds the perfect seed, Aunt thinks she can recreate a plant that has been extinct for thousands of years. If she really can do this, the possibilities are endless . . .

'Wow,' I say, wishing I could think of something clever to say. But Aunt isn't listening to me. She is holding a vial up to the porthole window.

'Nothing is growing yet,' she says, almost to herself. She turns to me. 'There have been famines and shortages of food before and there will be again. You read books. I assume you know about the times bad weather or disease wiped out crops or war impeded the distribution of food.'

I nod furiously. I have read about such things in

Father's newspaper, when his back was turned.

'You are right about seeds, Nico,' she continues, carefully returning the vial to its wooden rack. 'They are the future. I can only think that you have some of my genes.'

'I do, Aunt, I do! More than the usual twenty-five per cent shared between an aunt and her niece. I'm *sure* of it.'

Aunt smiles and I'm sure that I see a twinkle in her eyes, somewhere behind those huge glasses of hers.

'I suppose,' she says slowly, 'I could write a letter to your parents and let them know you are safe.'

My heart starts to race. It's as though storm clouds have parted after a long period of darkness and the sun is shining brightly, making anything feel possible.

'I don't think my parents will care that I've gone, Aunt.'

She holds up her hand. 'It's the best thing – the kindest

thing – to do, Nico.'

'Very well,' I say. 'Perhaps you could write the letter right now?'

Before you change your mind.

'I am the hardest worker in the world,' I add, with zero evidence to prove that fact. 'And a very fast learner.'

To my surprise, Aunt sits back down, dips a quill in the ink and begins to write quickly in an elaborate hand.

Once she has finished, she hands it to me.

Brother,

Nico is safe with me, aboard Anthos. I believe she can benefit from some education and some hard work. I suggest she remains on the ship until I see fit to send her home. Here, with me, her passion for science can be encouraged.

Regards,

Dr. R. Hamilton.

'Perfect', I say, grinning.

'There should be a mail box on the road near the beach in Cuckmere Haven. I've been studying a local map in the last few days to fully understand the lie of the land and I'd say it's probably a two-hour round trip, maybe less. If the letter is intercepted, "R. Hamilton" could just as easily be Uncle Raymond,' she explains, taking a stick of sealing wax and carefully melting one end in the candle flickering on her desk. The wax drips slowly on to the back of the envelope and, when the wax has sealed the envelope and is still warm, she removes the signet ring from her little finger and presses it firmly into the wax.

I watch her seal the envelope – and, at the same time, seal my fate. I think of the illustration she drew in my notebook.

Feeling slightly more confident I say, 'You said even scientists can dream . . .'

'I will admit that I too am intrigued by the Tree of Hope,' Aunt Ruth says carefully. 'I am usually dismissive of myths, but I think there might be some truth in this particular one.' She pauses. 'If the tree was in fruit all the year round, think of the possibilities. We could one day recreate the tree – and many others like it – and end world hunger. Let me speak, Nico. Scientists must never be excitable. As I was saying, a tree consistently bearing an excessive amount of fruit would have attracted all sorts of birds. Which means . . .'

'The seeds were dispersed in their poo . . . I mean dung!' I hop from one foot to the other. 'Can we go to Sicily? Can we look for the fossilised dung, Aunt? *Please?*'

'Slow down, Nico,' Aunt says. 'I am thinking.'

I stare at her, trying to work out what is going on in that incredible brain of hers.

'If you look in the last few pages of the notebook, you will see that I have made some further notes . . .'

I flick through the back of the notebook and, sure enough, there are a series of incomprehensible scribbles and equations and notes. Finally, I reach a single page with a series of words separated by arrows.

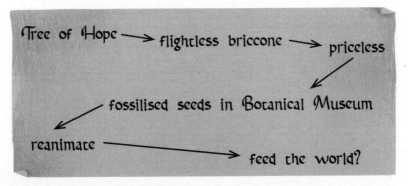

'Wow,' I say. 'So you *do* believe in the Tree of Hope?'

'I do believe the *briccone* existed and that the tree from which it ate bore fruit of immense value—'

'Magical fruit?'

'I'm not sure I believe in magic, Nico. But the fruit might be of considerable scientific value and as such could be used for my experiment. But' – and she holds up a hand to stop me from interrupting again – 'I would like you and Matteo to look for some fossilised seeds on the beach at Cuckmere Haven. Even if we do decide to go to Sicily, I still have research to do and I would like to be sure that I really am on the cusp of making a proper breakthrough. I also have to remind you that I can't afford to pay the crew to sail that far. Having said all of that, the Tree of Hope could be the most valuable tree in the world, should it turn out to be real. So we shouldn't discuss it with anyone who isn't on *Anthos*.' Goosebumps ripple down my arms. 'Do you understand?'

I nod. She hands me the letter before turning back to her huge book. 'And, Nico. Don't forget that above all else you must continue to protect my identity as a woman. Can you do that?'

'Yes! I can! Thank you for trusting me, Aunt,' I say, but she doesn't respond. She is engrossed in her work and my time with her is up.

I shut the door quietly behind me, notebook in hand, and look up once more at the Siberian salt staining the stairs. The sky is vast and blue and, this time, it feels as though the possibilities are endless.

10

I run up the stairs two at a time and bump straight into the captain, who is taking in the view of Cuckmere Haven. To the west is a row of four cottages perching on the cliff. To the east is a river snaking gently inland and then, as far as the eye can see, the Seven Sisters looking out to Europe. The chalky cliffs are such a brilliant, dazzling white that I have to shield my eyes with my hand. Imagine the fossils in those cliffs, on that beach!

'The Sisters are glorious, aren't they?' says the captain, turning around and flashing his generous smile.

'I've never seen such a *pure* white,' I say.

'Yes, they are pristine,' he says, leaning on the railing and gazing back at the cliffs. 'Each of the seven cliffs has a name. As do the dips *between* each cliff. The first cliff is called Haven Brow and its dip is Short Bottom. The second . . . I don't remember. The third is Rough Brow and Rough Bottom. There are many bottoms.'

Many bottoms!

I have to cough to stop myself from laughing.

'Are you ready?' shouts Matteo from the other end of the ship.

'Nearly!' I shout. 'Dr Hamilton says I can stay a little longer, captain.'

'The boys will be pleased,' he says, patting my arm. 'Now, don't keep them waiting.'

I rush to my cabin and find Astra curled up in a tight ball, utterly unaware of the world outside. She seems to have grown sturdier in the short time since she led me on to the ship, or perhaps last night's fish supper strengthened her. She looks up at me adoringly. I can't bear to leave her here, so I put the notebook and pencil in my bag, in case I need to do some quick sketches on the beach, and tuck Astra under my arm.

Etienne is already in the rowing boat and Matteo is waiting by the ladder. He frowns when he sees Astra. 'Must you bring her?'

'Yes I must. I have a letter from Dr Hamilton!' I say, waving it around. 'It's to my father, telling him that I am safely aboard *Anthos* and will be staying for a while. Etienne, would you post it while we are on the beach?'

'Of course!' shouts Etienne from the boat. 'That is excellent.'

'It *is* good news,' says Matteo, grinning. 'You seem to learn quickly, so you might even be some use around the ship! So long as no one finds out there's a girl on board. But . . .' He looks at Astra again.

'She'll cause no fuss, I promise.'

Matteo looks sceptical, but he takes Astra as I climb down the ladder and then he passes her carefully to me. She wriggles at the sight of all that sea stretching out around her, but I take her firmly by the scruff of her neck and put her on my knee.

'Nice bag,' says Etienne, nodding at my puffin bag.

'You would have done a much better job,' I say, smiling.

'I doubt it. Embroidery is not my thing.' He points at a bucket. 'There are some tools for you and Matteo.'

Matteo clambers to the front of the rowing boat. Stroking Astra rhythmically to calm her down, I spot a chisel, paint brushes large and small and a magnifying glass. I have wanted to use those tools to excavate the past since I saw illustrations of them in one of the twins' books about dinosaur bones and I feel excitement swell in my chest. Still, I don't imagine Matteo and Etienne want to hear me discuss chisels at length.

As Etienne rows methodically towards the foreshore, the sweat on his back slowly spreads until his shirt is soaked through. He pushes the oars tirelessly through the water as though they are merely matchsticks, although I know they must be heavy. Matteo points his telescope straight at the shore, while I balance on the tiny seat at the back of the boat, my bag at my feet, Astra on my knee. She seems to have acclimatised to the sea and doesn't even seem to mind the occasional splash of water; in fact, she is hypnotised by Etienne's rhythmical rowing, her tiny head following the circular motion of the oars.

Clouds scurry past overhead, obscuring the sun. The vista in front of us is vast. I look slowly from left to right, from west to east. To the far left, according to the captain's nautical chart, is Hope Point. Next, perched at the top of a cliff, the row of coastguard cottages. Then there is Cuckmere River, flowing straight out to sea, its many tributaries coiling away and forming small lakes. And, finally, the Seven Sisters cliffs, rising out of the ground like giant icebergs.

What did the captain say the first of the Seven Sisters cliffs was called? Ah yes, Haven Brow – and its dip, Short Bottom. How could I forget! The first section of Haven Brow runs in a straight line, then there is a zigzag section of cliffs that form a series of small beaches. As I gaze at the Seven Sisters, the sun elbows the clouds away and the cliffs burn bright white again.

Matteo angles the telescope to the beach below the coastguard cottages.

'Why are there sheds on wheels at the edge of the sea?' he says, turning to look at me, as though I am the authority on everything that exists on land.

'Let me have a look,' I say.

Matteo hands the telescope to me, poking it beneath one of Etienne's arms as he circles forwards. 'Don't drop it in the sea.'

I look through the telescope and see nothing but blue. The sky. Nothing but white. The cliffs. Finally, I manage to focus on the cottages and lower the lens till I see the beach. There, at the water's edge, is a row of five small wooden cabins on wheels, each with wooden stairs. Young maids sit on the stairs, holding towels and long, flowing cloaks for their rich employers. In the shallows of the water, older women stand in long flannel gowns, looking anxious as the waves break gently over their ankles.

'Those aren't sheds,' I say, leaning forward and returning the telescope to Matteo. 'They are bathing machines. The women sitting on the steps are "dippers" and the women in the water are . . . bathers, I suppose. Have you never seen people go for a swim before?'

'Of course I have, but not wearing a gown,' he replies.

'Sea bathing is very fashionable, you know,' I say. 'Doctors say it has great health benefits. Especially when the sea is cold.'

'They look ridiculous,' says Etienne. 'Anyway, we are here now, as close as we can get to the cliffs.'

He pulls off his boots and socks, jumps out of the boat and drags the hull into shallow water. I take my boots and socks off too, tuck Astra into the bag, with her head peeping out, and climb carefully out of the boat, into the clear sea.

'The water is freezing!' I shout. I scramble on to the pebble beach and put my socks and boots on again.

Matteo and Etienne look at me with a 'what-did-you-expect?' stare.

And then Matteo's legs wobble, his arms thrash about and he falls to his knees. His face is as pale as the chalk cliffs behind him.

'*Mal de debarquement*,' says Etienne, pushing the boat right on to the beach.

'What?' I ask, trying to pull Matteo up. But Matteo drops my hand and shakes his head.

'Leave him for a minute,' says Etienne. 'His body thinks it's still on the ship and it needs to acclimatise to being on land. He will feel his body swaying even if it's not.'

'You mean he has to get his . . . land legs?' I ask, laughing.

Etienne nods, but his expression is serious. 'He'll get over it soon enough.' He takes the rope attached to the hull of the boat and ties it around a large rock, before piling several other rocks on top. 'Just in case; the tide is starting to turn and it'll be pretty far out by the time I'm back. The three of us can carry the boat back out to the sea if necessary.'

I take Astra out of my bag and set her down on the pebbly beach. She tentatively places a paw on the stones and then she's off, running around in ever-increasing circles, as though she has been waiting for this moment all of her short life.

'Here's the letter,' I say, pulling it out of my bag. 'The round trip shouldn't take longer than two hours.' Etienne takes the letter, tucks it into his back trouser pocket and turns to look at the path leading north, away from the beach and towards the road, where Dr Hamilton was sure there would be a mail box.

'Hang on a second, Etienne,' I say. 'If you see some good-quality soil, rich in nutrients, can you put it in this seed bag? I'll explain later.'

He stuffs it in a coat pocket. 'Good luck with the fossil hunting.'

'Thank you,' Matteo and I say in unison.

He sets off with long, determined strides. I sit next to Matteo on the sharp pebbles, shifting my bottom around until I am as comfortable as I will ever be, and listen to the sea. The hiss and fizz of small waves hitting the shore and the drag when the waves pull pebbles back out with them.

hiss fizz drag hiss fizz drag hiss fizz

'Nico!'

Matteo is tugging at my sleeve. 'The sea has put you in a trance! We're not on holiday; Dr Hamilton has sent us here to work.'

'Of course,' I say. 'Well someone is feeling better!'

Matteo is laying out our tools for the fossil hunt,

so that I can have first refusal. I take a hammer and chisel, a brush and a small magnifying glass and put them in the battered wooden bucket Etienne pointed out on the boat.

'The bread is for later,' says Matteo, smiling as I pull off a small corner to eat.

'That's mean,' I say, pretending to be serious. 'But fair enough. Let's go to the far end of the beach where the cliff sticks out into the sea. Then we can walk back towards the boat.'

Matteo nods and we walk in silence, occasionally looking up at the towering cliffs to our left or out to sea to our right. Astra lags behind, the smaller pebbles too tricky for her delicate paws to navigate until, eventually, I put her back in the bag so that she doesn't miss out on the view but doesn't have to make any kind of effort.

'You spoil her,' he says.

'I love her,' I say, smiling. 'Matteo, what do you

know about fossils?'

He shrugs. 'A bit. I know that they are the surviving part of plants and animals that have been preserved in rock. I know that fossils can tell us about the world the plant or animal used to live in . . .'

My heart swells. He knows stuff! He *is* interested. I could take the warm hand of my new friend and squeeze it tight, but I know that might be a bit much for him.

He is still going. '. . . I know that the rings on a tree trunk show you its age. I know that amber is fossilised tree resin. Dr Hamilton lent me a book when I was having nightmares on the way to Siberia.'

'What were your nightmares about?'

'Not much. Storms. Pirates. Mother. That kind of thing.'

His mother. I don't know what to say, so I talk quickly to fill the awkward silence.

'Did you know that the Earth is 4.5 billion years old? My brothers had a book about the Sussex coastline and

I'm pretty sure the ecosystem here in Cuckmere Haven dates back to the Cretaceous period. That is to say, 145 to 66 million years ago – basically the period in which dinosaurs became extinct and the first flowering plants appeared. I reckon there will be lots of echinoids on the beach. Sorry – sea urchins. And sponges. Bivalves. Look out for belemnites that are as minuscule as your fingernail. Tiny, tiny squids, but with a hard skeleton. So, not *really* like squid. The chalk is made up of the skeletal remains of planktonic algae known as . . .'

'Do you think we should stop talking and start looking?' asks Matteo. But he's smiling at me. I don't think he minds me being a chatterbox.

I set Astra free again – exhausted, she curls up in a tight ball on top of a big rock and is asleep before you could count to one. I crouch down on my haunches. 'Yes, yes, work. Right. We'd better not get too close to the cliffs, in case the loose rock falls on us, but we can have a go at this lower section of white cliff leading to the sea. See this flint pebble with random white stripes on it, that looks as though it's been painted? They are fragments of an inoceramid bivalve shell.'

Matteo leans towards me and traces the white stripes with the tip of one finger. 'It's beautiful. Is that what Dr Hamilton wants us to look for?'

'Dr Hamilton wants us to find fossilised bird dung containing seeds,' I say. 'I'm not sure we'll find them, not here. We'd have to be extremely lucky. But we shouldn't go back to the ship empty-handed because then our trip will be regarded as a failure. So I think we should bring back anything we find that seems interesting.'

'How about we do some chiselling?' asks Matteo, his eyes bright.

'We can try!' I angle the chisel at 45 degrees, as the diagrams in my book about fossils and seeds illustrated, and start to hit it gently with the hammer. A piece of chalky rock falls away easily. I tap the piece of rock softly. There, beneath the dust of time, sits a crinoid. I am the first person to ever see it. It's been sitting here, encased in chalk, since the Paleozoic era, which was . . . I try to visualise the page in my book. Yes! I remember. Five hundred and forty-five to 248 million years ago. It's very, very, very old. Like some kind of time machine that can connect the distant past to the present. Oh, the stories it could tell!

'What is it?' asks Matteo.

I realise that, for once, I have managed to keep my thoughts to myself, as I nearly always did at home. Perhaps, with time, I will learn what to say out loud and what I should keep in my head.

'A sea lily, I think.'

'We found a fossilised plant!'

Matteo shouts, his dimple showing for the first time today.

'Actually . . . it's an invertebrate. It used its feathery arms to filter food from the seawater. Look, you can see its stem, which helped it attach itself to hard surfaces, and its arms, all bunched together. It does look like a plant though, you're right.'

As I note down the location of the crinoid in my leather notebook, Matteo angles his chisel and starts to **tap tap tap** at the chalk.

Just then, there's a loud rumble behind us and a blur of white, before an almighty crash several feet along from where we are kneeling. A rock, as big as a human head, lands. It splits open and splinters of chalk fly through the air.

I scoop up Astra, grab Matteo, and we run to the sea's edge. Matteo is still stumbling as we run.

We stop, breathing hard, and stare up to the top of the cliff, but the sun is too bright, the cliffs too white. We can't see anything.

'Did someone throw a rock at us?' Matteo whispers.

'I don't know,' I say.

We look upwards for a few minutes, shielding our eyes with our hands.

'It's probably just natural rockfall,' I say, eventually. 'Perhaps we should stick to looking for pebbles with fossils in them rather than excavating the actual cliff.'

I turn to Matteo and see his face is as white as the cliffs again.

'You've got chalk all over your face!' I say, laughing.

He shows me his white palms. He laughs and I then laugh too and it's a relief, because *what if someone was aiming that rock at us?* He cups some seawater in his hands and splashes his face clean and then points at the retreating sea. 'Nico. Look. The tide is going out. Why don't you take Astra and check the other side of the cliff for fossils while I walk slowly back towards the boat. If I find anything interesting, I'll put it in my bucket and we can sort through everything back at the rowing boat while we

wait for Etienne.'

11

The pebbles on the other side of the cliff appear to be a similar mix of flint and chalk and stone. Astra sits on a large, dry rock and holds her head up to the sun, her eyes squeezed tightly shut.

I get down on my hands and knees and methodically search through the stones, to see if they have any unusual patterns on them. I tap on them to see if they have been home to a trilobite or a bivalve. Sometimes I just like the look of a stone. Some are sedimentary rock, like the bright white chalk that occasionally has a perfect round hole in it – when I hold it up to the sky, the hole becomes an intense blue. Or metamorphic rock, like the grey slate that is formed of multiple layers. These particular stones are smooth and sparkly or rough and lined. Each and every one has a story, a history that goes back thousands and thousands of years.

As I trawl through the stones, I try to remember what the nickname is for the curved, blackened bivalves you sometimes find – ah yes, Devil's Toenails.

Astra hisses suddenly. I turn and see she is arching her back and her tail has fluffed up to twice its usual size.

'Silly cat,' I mutter. 'There's nothing to be scared of.'

She stares at the beach behind me and hisses again.

I stand up awkwardly, my back stiff from bending

over. I look to the east, towards the next section of cliff. Nothing there. To the west, *Anthos* is still bobbing about in the distance. There are other boats, but much further away, almost as far away as France.

'There's nothing to worry about,' I reassure her. I get back down on my hands and knees and start shifting through the stones again, putting the most promising-looking ones in the bucket; I'm sure one or two will reveal interesting fossils later, even if they are not specifically what Aunt wants.

'You ran away from me.'

The voice is quiet, barely above a whisper. I spin around. The boy with black curly hair is standing above me, his hands resting on his narrow hips. I didn't notice what he was wearing at Emsworth, but now, in the bright sunlight, I see everything. A shirt that was once white but is now grey, untucked. A blue sailor's jacket, with two of the three gold buttons missing, that is too big for him; the shoulders fall almost as far down as his elbows. His blue trousers have been cut off at the ankles and loose threads dangle over brown, unlaced boots. His right eye twitches, which I take as a bad case of nerves, despite his bold stance.

I look over his shoulder at the tide going out and realise that enough sand has been revealed for him to creep swiftly and silently along from the next bay.

I wipe my dusty hands casually on my trousers. 'Have we met?'

'You remember.'

'I have to go,' I say, putting my tools in the bucket. He takes a step forward. I step sideways so that I am between the boy and Astra, whose tail is twisting around furiously. We are doing our strange dance again.

'I know who you are,' he says slowly. 'You shouldn't be on *Anthos*. You are breaking the law. No girls or women allowed on ships.'

My blood runs cold. 'If that's the law then I am happy to break it. And you are an ignorant fool.'

He takes another step towards me. He is scrawny, but he might still throw a good punch. He doesn't know that I grew up with twin brothers, though, and can more than fend for myself.

'I know about Dr Hamilton's research,' he says. 'Anything for me in that bag?'

My head is light, my legs wobbly. As though I too haven't got my land legs.

I swallow hard, push my shoulders back and lift my chin slightly. I have to look as tall and fearless as I can.

In my bag is the notebook. My drawing of the Tree of Hope. A map of the botanical garden. Aunt Ruth's equations, revealing that the fossilised seeds from the Tree of Hope might really have existed and are of vital importance to her research. It was a mistake to bring it to

the beach. He must never see my drawings. He must never know that such a magical tree once existed and might still.

A shiver passes through my body, as though my spine is now a thin spike of ice.

'The bag is for the kitten,' I say. 'She's too small to walk far.'

He laughs, but it's a cruel sound, as though he's mocking me. 'The very same cat you chose over me. When I asked for help. Not very kind.'

Well you weren't very kind to the leather merchant, I think, but I don't say anything.

Even if he's a crook, I don't want to be mean. 'I'm sorry,' I say, lifting Astra up with one hand and the bucket in the other. 'Are you still in trouble?'

'Depends,' he says. 'I will be in gigantic trouble if I go back empty-handed.'

'Nico!'

It's Matteo, impatiently calling my name in the distance.

'I really do have to go,' I say, forcing a smile that no doubt looks more like a scowl.

He suddenly grabs my forearm and grips it tightly. Up close, his eyes are the same dark green as the seaweed undulating in the shallow water.

'Tell me about the research!' he says, his breath hot and sour. 'Or I will tell everyone who will listen that you are a girl on a ship. Do you want to end up in prison?'

I vigorously shake his hand off my arm and quickly put the puffin bag into the bucket with the stones and the implements and scoop Astra up.

I feel sick, but I am angry above anything else. How dare this wild boy tell me I can't be a member of crew on board a scientific voyage? He is just jealous.

I move towards him, thrusting Astra in his direction. She hisses and extends her claws. 'I dare you to threaten me again, Otis King.'

'Nico!'

Matteo's voice is closer.

Otis looks behind me, his eyes wide.

It's now or never.

Holding tightly on to Astra and the bucket, I turn and run awkwardly across the uneven pebbles, until I reach the sand at the edge of the sea.

I stop and turn. Otis is standing on the beach, an eyebrow raised. I can't read his expression, but does he look amused?

'You will never triumph,' I shout, but the wind carries my words away.

*

'Nico!'

I run around the cliff and bump straight into Matteo, almost knocking him over.

'Now you look as though *you've* seen a ghost,' says Matteo.

'No,' I gasp, panting so hard that I can barely get the words out. 'The pirate boy.'

'Calm down,' he says, taking hold of my hands and gripping them firmly. 'Who exactly did you see?' I am still trying to catch my breath. 'Come and sit down.'

We walk slowly towards the rowing boat, which, now

that the tide has gone out, is stranded on a series of spherical chalky rocks.

'Why do those rocks look like heads?' I ask.

Matteo laughs. 'Goodness, Nico, what just happened to you? I thought you knew everything there was to know about rocks.'

'Not *everything*,' I say, smiling.

We sit on the sand, side by side, looking out to sea. Astra gallops up and down, skidding to a halt every now and again and lifting a sandy paw in disgust. I keep staring towards the beach where I met Otis King, but Matteo distracts me by showing me how to skim flat stones across the shallow water.

'Otis King came out of nowhere,' I say. 'With his wild curly hair and his odd clothes and his eyes like seaweed.'

Matteo nods gravely.

'You knew it was him in the fog this morning, didn't you?' I ask.

'I wasn't sure,' says Matteo, throwing a large flat stone that skips six, seven times. 'It's very easy to be misled by fog. It's full of shapes and shadows. But now I'm sure it was him. I should know by now that he and his father are never too far away, especially near the English coast. They are desperate to be paid that handsome sum of money by the scientists in London.'

'Why?' I ask. 'Why do they need the money so badly?'

Matteo shakes his head, picks up a large rock and throws it at one of the head-shaped rocks. The large rock smashes into smithereens, but the head-shaped rock remains intact.

'Oh,' he says, pulling a face. 'I didn't mean to be so destructive!'

'Hang on,' I say. I walk across the head-shaped rocks, careful not to slip on the remnants of wispy seaweed that cover the tops like hair, and pick up a large fragment of the smashed rock. I study it for a while. It can't be. But it is!

'My goodness, Matteo!' I lift the fragment up for him to see. 'I think you did it! I think there are fossilised seeds in this rock!'

'Show me!' shouts Matteo, jumping up.

I run back through the rock pools, no longer caring about getting my boots wet.

'Pass me a magnifying glass,' I say. 'These could be Early Cretaceous angiosperm seeds, Matteo! An actual dinosaur might have trodden on them!'

I examine the piece of rock through the magnifying glass. It looks like a pine cone carved out of stone. A very, very old pine cone.

Matteo puts his hand out and I give it to him. 'Do you think this is what Dr Hamilton needs for his research?' he asks.

'I don't know,' I say. 'I wish Etienne would hurry. I'm worried Otis King will come back.'

Matteo's face clouds over. 'What if Otis and his father

try to board *Anthos* while we're on the beach?'

'They wouldn't dare,' I say. 'Besides, we would be able to see them from the beach.'

Matteo looks through his telescope, east towards the bay where Otis confronted me, and then straight out to sea. 'We should still keep an eye on *Anthos* and be ready to row back. I wonder where Etienne has got to . . .'

We wait impatiently for Etienne, pulling at chunks of bread as the tide comes back in and covers the stone heads. The sun colours the sky orange and red as it drops towards the horizon. Matteo walks up the steep bank of stones on the beach and towards the path, to see if Etienne is on his way.

'I can see him in the distance!' Matteo shouts. He wobbles unsteadily back down the bank and wraps the rest of the bread back up in a piece of clean cloth – the sleeve of an old shirt – and drops it into his bucket.

'What took you so long?' I ask Etienne as he

slides down the bank of stones on his bottom. He looks exhausted.

'I stopped to get your soil, but then I got distracted,' he says, sheepishly. He takes a piece of paper out of his pocket and shows us a drawing of the river winding inland, with two herons sitting regally at the edge of the water. Matteo and I look at each other and silently vow not to break Etienne's happiness with news of the pirate boy. Not just yet . . .

'You have got a real talent,' I say. 'Did you post my letter?'

He smiles and nods.

'No turning back now, Nico,' says Matteo, grinning at me. 'You're stuck with me and Etienne.'

*

While Matteo and Etienne haul the rowing boat out of the water and back on to *Anthos*, I take the buckets of fossils and stones back to my cold cabin with Astra and light the stove. Astra winds herself around my legs, looking up at me with huge eyes – it's funny how cats have evolved to encourage their humans to feed them on demand – but I have no food to give her. 'Hopefully later, Astra.'

It occurs to me that if now I am staying on *Anthos* for the foreseeable future, it is time to earn my keep. I empty the stones out of the buckets and lay them out carefully on my old summer dress, next to the hammers, chisels and magnifying glasses. I tip some of the soil Etienne gave me into each bucket and carefully dot radish, red pepper and salad seeds as close together as I dare, so that the seedlings, when they push up, don't try to steal each other's space. I cover them with another layer of soil, pat the surface down gently and divide the rainwater from Astra's bowl between the buckets. I will put the buckets in a sunny corner of the ship and hope that, with plenty of sun and rain, we shall have an abundance of fiery radishes, sweet peppers and bright green salad leaves in around three weeks' time.

Now that the stones from the beach have dried out, they look a lot less appealing, especially the sparkling jet-black stones which have turned a dull, lifeless grey. It's as though they have lost their magic. But it's not what they look like that matters – it's what they might be hiding.

I don't bother trying to split open the smallest stones, but I put them to one side because they remind me of tiny black seeds. The bigger ones I bash with the hammer, but they reveal nothing, not even an ammonite. Thank goodness for the fossilised pine cone! I will eat with Matteo and Etienne and then take the pine cone to Aunt, who is no doubt expecting a report on our beach finds tonight. A proper scientist would log all her finds in a notebook, I think, so I reach inside my bag. The only thing I pull out is orange cat hairs.

My throat tightens. The notebook is gone.

My heart **thud thud thuds** in my chest.

I check my trouser pockets. Nothing.

'No!' I shout, so loudly that Astra opens her eyes and stares at me, disgusted with me for not respecting her nap time.

It can't be. I turn the bag upside down. A few grains of sand fall out. Nothing else. This time it really was Otis, I think. He stole the notebook from my bag before I knew he was there.

I swallow hard. I feel sick – sicker than I did during the storm or even when I heard Father say he was going to confiscate everything. Because this isn't just about me. It's about Aunt Ruth's life's work. I pick Astra up and hold her tightly against my chest, to steady my thumping heart. 'What if . . . what if the Pirate Kings get there first? What if *they* are the ones to find the fossilised Tree of Hope seeds?'

12

There is only one possible way out of this: we have to sail to Sicily. But first I must show Aunt what we found on the beach.

I walk quickly towards Aunt Ruth's cabin, but I am stopped by Matteo, who is with his father.

'Tell Papà who you saw today,' he says gently.

I take a deep breath. 'I was in a small bay that was hidden from the main stretch of beach, looking for fossils, and Otis King appeared out of nowhere. He threatened to tell everyone willing to listen that there's a girl on the ship.'

The captain tugs at his beard. 'I don't like the sound of that. At all. There are six of us – well, five, I can't really count Dr Hamilton as his head is always in a book – and only two of the Kings. But they are, as you say, desperate. And Mr King is as cunning as a fox. I will speak to Dr Hamilton now . . .'

'There's something else.' I gulp. 'Otis stole my notebook. There was a drawing of the Tree of Hope inside, and a sketch I did the other night of the botanical garden in Palermo *and* the locked room your *nonna* told you about. And recently Dr Hamilton added an illustration of a fossilised seed. And . . . he made all these notes at the back of the notebook in which he concluded that the Tree of Hope really existed and its fossilised seeds are therefore priceless. ' I can feel the tears pricking at my eyes. 'I think Otis and his father might realise that the tree is important. Maybe they're already on their way to Sicily and it's all my fault.'

'In that case,' says the captain, sounding rather stern but putting his hand on my arm and squeezing it to try and calm me down, 'we really must call a meeting with Dr Hamilton. I will go and knock on his door now and invite him to supper.'

'No,' I say miserably. 'I'll go and ask him myself.'

This is my mess to sort out. I can't expect the captain to act on my behalf. I'm not a baby.

But as soon as I arrive at Aunt Ruth's door, I feel sick with nerves again. It feels as though the ship is sailing through a storm, even though she is still anchored in the bay at Cuckmere Haven.

This time I can see Aunt Ruth's magnified eye peering through the spy hole in her cabin door.

She opens the door and ushers me inside. 'What news do you have for me, Nico?'

'Matteo found this, Aunt,' I say, handing her the fossilised pine cone. Might as well give her the good news first.

She puts it carefully on her desk, next to a lantern, and examines it with a large magnifying glass.

She gasps. That must be a good sign!

I wait for her to finish examining it. 'This is an excellent Jurassic fossil,' she says. 'This cone obviously grew in wet conditions, because the pine scales curve upwards, as though to protect the seeds. If the conditions had been dry, the scales would be downward facing and the seeds would have dispersed efficiently in the wind.'

'Might it be useful for your experiment?' I ask tentatively.

'I am not sure. I am going to remove a few pine seeds and see if they are in reasonable condition. I should know quickly if they are viable.'

I stand behind her, looking at the scientific graffiti on the walls and waiting for her to decide if the seeds are useful or not.

'Hmmmm,' says Aunt.

'Yes?' I ask.

'Unfortunately, these seeds haven't fossilised very well because of the wet conditions in which the pine cone existed. I will have to discuss the possibily of Sicily with the captain and his crew.'

'Aunt . . . I have something to say.' She looks at me impatiently.

My words won't come. I am unable to confess.

'The captain has called an urgent meeting and you are invited to supper,' I say at last.

I expect her to turn the invite down, but she simply nods and says that she will see me later.

*

I put the buckets of planted seeds in a sunny, sheltered and secret corner of the ship. I offer to help Etienne catch the fish for our supper. I tidy up the already tidy galley. I ask Matteo if I can cut the bread or clean the sparkling deck. I unfold and fold the blankets in the sick bay. Anything to distract myself. Etienne lights the stove in the galley and cooks the fish. Finally, Aunt Ruth appears and for the first time we all sit at a long wooden table in the galley – nothing as informal as sitting around a fire cross-legged for Dr Hamilton.

I can't look at her. I have to remember not to call her 'Aunt' *and* I have to confess that I have messed everything up. It's strange to see Matteo and Etienne looking at my aunt with admiration – even the captain and Claude are respectful of her, giving her a plate of the most tender part of the fish and the middle of the loaf rather than the slightly stale ends.

Matteo nudges me and looks across the table at Dr Hamilton.

'Dr Hamilton,' I say. 'I have something to tell you.' But then I don't say anything.

'Spit it out, Nico,' she says.

'So,' I say. 'Um. Today. On the beach. The pirate boy. He stole my . . .'

'Pirate boy? What are you talking about?'

Matteo looks at me kindly, encouraging me. Everyone else puts their cutlery down.

I push away my untouched plate of food. 'Otis King, son of Mr King, was spying on me on the beach this afternoon and he stole my leather notebook with my drawing of the Tree of Hope in it. And also, the map of the botanical garden and your thoughts about the Tree of Hope and its value to the world . . .'

'I see,' she says, very calmly. And she pops another piece of white fish in her mouth.

Be cross with me, shout at me, but don't sit in silence, I think. It's much, much worse when grown-ups are silently disappointed. I open my mouth again, but no words follow. I close it in defeat.

'Is there anything else?' my aunt says.

'You aren't in trouble, Nico,' says Claude kindly, pushing at his blond hair till it is pretty much all standing on end. 'It's best you speak up if you have something important to say, but remember we are all on your side.'

'We really are,' says Etienne, smiling at his father.

I have never received this kind of loyalty and encouragement before and I am surprised by how quickly the courage surges through me. 'The Kings will now know how important the Tree of Hope was. And its seeds, which might well be in the botanical garden, if the captain's *nonna* was right about the locked room. Perhaps they are already be on their way to Palermo,' I say. And then, somehow, I am on my feet and speaking loudly and clearly, with everyone looking at me. 'But . . . we could get there first. We could leave right now. The captain knows the way, after all. And I would love to go. So, so much. Can you imagine if we could actually find some fossilised seeds from the Tree of Hope? Your research would be complete and we could end famine, just like Santa Lucia!'

Aunt chews her food for a long time, as though savouring every last mouthful. 'I have to admit that I have always wanted to visit the volcano in Sicily. I've seen some wonderful drawings of Mount Etna. So . . .' It feels as though she is tormenting me, but I'm sure she is just mapping out ideas in her head. She looks at Matteo's father. 'Captain. Let's make a deal. If you are willing to sail to Palermo, I can pay you no extra wages but, in return, you will have the opportunity to see your family and show off your rather fine son.'

Matteo beams. I have never seen his dimple so pronounced.

Aunt smiles back at him. She looks younger when she relaxes, much younger than thirty. 'I must admit that I have had enough of pottering around England for now. I quite fancy a trip to Europe. Better weather, better

food and, one hopes, better seeds.'

'Well,' says the captain. 'Such unexpected – but welcome – news. It goes without saying that Matteo and I are very keen to go to Sicily. However, I realise that this is not the voyage Claude and Etienne signed up for. I am happy to accept no extra wages, but what do *you* think, Claude?'

Claude scratches his head more vigorously, flattening his hair in the process. 'Etienne, would you like to meet your maternal grandmother in Marseille?'

Etienne grins. 'Really? I have always tried to draw her, but it's so hard when I've never met her . . .'

Claude turns to the captain. 'If we sail with you to Sicily, will you sail back via Marseille and drop us off? I know it's out of your way, but a favour deserves a favour.'

'I don't see why not,' says the captain. 'I will work out the journey in my cabin tonight. Matteo, Etienne, Nico – Claude and I will call on you should we need you for specific jobs. Otherwise, your chores are pretty straightforward: keep the decks clean, keep the sails in perfect condition and keep the food coming. You must also take it in turns to keep watch. We know how devious the Kings can be and we cannot risk them getting anywhere near *Anthos*.'

'We won't let them!' Matteo and I say in unison.

'No way!' says Etienne, a fraction of a second later.

The captain waves his hands around, motioning us away. 'Right, *ragazzi*, why are you all still here? Go to bed and get a good night's sleep. *Sogni d'oro*! Sweet dreams! We are about to set sail on the voyage of a lifetime!'

I turn to see Aunt's reaction – but she has already snuck back to her cabin.

13

10 April 1832

I wake at dawn and open the shutter on my porthole window. Astra squints at the unexpected brightness before curling up again and hiding her face between her front paws.

I almost have to pinch myself: here I am on Aunt's ship, exceeding my wildest dreams and about to sail through Europe to Sicily! I can barely believe it. I want to share my excitement with someone and it's clearly not going to be Astra, so I put the map my aunt gave me all those years ago in my pocket, pull on a jumper and wander onto the deck.

There is no sign of Matteo or Etienne, but Claude is checking the sails thoroughly for rips, his face stiff with concentration. The sun has disappeared and the sea is drab today.

I unfold the map and lay it out on the deck.

'I see you came prepared,' says the captain. 'Did you know when you ran away from home that you were going to sail across Europe?'

'Of course not,' I say, smiling. 'But I didn't want to stay in Sussex my whole life.'

'Let me show you the route I intend to take,' he says, balancing elegantly on his haunches and putting his finger on East Sussex. 'We shall sail west from Cuckmere Haven till the end of the Channel and then south through the Bay of Biscay. Past the west coast of Portugal, before turning sharply east right here and into the Strait of Gibraltar. Then we shall sail through the Alboran Sea and, finally, the Mediterranean. I'd say that's around

2,500 nautical miles and, with favourable wind, it should take us just under four weeks.'

I still feel as though I am dreaming. When the captain goes off to haul the anchor into the chain locker, I trace the route with my forefinger again and again. This is what I have dreamed of my whole life, but I never, ever thought it would actually happen. The longer I am on *Anthos*, the more my old life – at home, alone in my room with my embroidery, longing for more science books, desperate for a friend – is losing its sharpness.

A gust of wind lifts my map up into the air and I have to use both hands to hold it down. Best, then, that I fold it up and put it away. I can't keep losing things or no one will trust me to do anything.

There is a clatter of plates and I go into the galley. I'm expecting to find Matteo, cleaning the plates one by one and stacking them neatly on the sideboard to drain. Instead, I am surprised to find Aunt Ruth boiling water on the stove for a cup of tea, reusing the tea leaves because we only have a small amount for the entire trip.

I sit at the table and lace and unlace my fingers. Every time I see her I have so many questions to ask, but I don't feel that I can because Otis stole the notebook yesterday and it's all my fault. I think that Aunt will take her tea back to her cabin without saying a word, but instead she sits down at the table opposite me.

'Good morning, Nico,' she says, sipping the hot, weak tea. 'Sorry I didn't offer to make you a cup.'

'It's fine; I don't much like the metallic taste of tea,' I say, which is true. I look out of the galley windows to see if anyone is around. Matteo and Etienne are busy stitching the minor rips in the sails that Claude has just noticed and I'm pretty sure they can't hear us in here.

'Why is my father so angry with you?'

Aunt puts her tea down. 'I thought you might ask about Solomon. I suspect it's because I won a scholarship to the local school and I was the only girl there. My parents expected Solomon to be the clever one, but it didn't quite work out that way. I don't think your father has ever forgiven me.'

Behind those huge glasses, there's a twinkle in her eyes. 'I don't think he's very impressed that I wear man's clothes on *Anthos*, nor has he ever bothered to find out why I have to sometimes pretend to be a male scientist. People don't always ask the right questions, Nico. They make judgements without finding out the truth.'

'He says you don't have any children because you work so hard. Is that true?'

Aunt reaches across the table and takes my hands. She holds them tightly and a shot of warmth travels through my body. 'It's not true. I would have loved a child. But it just wasn't to be.'

I would love to be your daughter, I think.

She squeezes my hands and then pulls them away and

stands up. 'Back to work for me, Nico. I am glad you are here. My job is sometimes terribly lonely and until you and the captain invited me for supper last night, I had all but forgotten what it was like to leave my cabin. But that doesn't mean I haven't got work to do. No doubt the boys could do with a hand with the sails.'

She is glad I am here! I want to cry with relief, with happiness.

Instead, I make a joke. 'I thought I'd left my life of sewing behind,' I say, pretending to be fed up.

'Ah yes, but you have to sew seeds to grow flowers,' says Aunt, quick as a flash and we both laugh and I realise that I never want to go home again.

*

As we sail south, towards Sicily, the air becomes warmer. We leave behind the murky brown English sea that looks like a cold cup of tea and push through water that is a more vivid, intense blue each day.

Aunt Ruth has given me a new notebook, bigger than the stolen one, and I try to think of all the shades of blue that could possibly describe the sea and the sky: azure, celeste, aqua, turquoise, navy. And, at night, when the sky is packed full of stars, midnight blue. I want to remember everything I see and taste and hear and feel on this voyage of discovery, from the blushed pink sunrises to the nip of salt in the air, to the roar of the seagulls, to the needles of soft rain.

I get up at dawn each day and water my seedlings with Astra winding in and out of my ankles. As my face and arms turn chestnut brown in the sun, so my seedlings become plants, reaching up for the sun, growing stronger each day. The growing conditions are perfect and soon we will be able to share bitter salad leaves, crunchy radishes and sweet red peppers.

Etienne, Matteo and I take it in turns to use the telescope to keep watch. Matteo suggests he toss a coin to see who should get up before dawn, but when he always chooses 'tails' and always wins, Etienne demands to see the coin. It's double-sided, with tails on both sides and Etienne feels cheated and tells Matteo that he must now keep watch at dawn for a straight week, whatever the weather. I start laughing and Etienne pulls a face, but then he starts laughing and Matteo can't help himself. Before long, we are collapsed in a heap in the middle of the deck and I look at them and think they are like my brothers, but in a good way.

Here on the ship, life is easy and uncomplicated and I am, for the first time in my life, happy.

14

1 May 1832

One day, when all the chores have been done and the sun has cooled a little, Matteo suggests the three of us play hide and seek. 'The only place that is out of bounds is Dr Hamilton's study,' he says.

I have never played before. I can't work out if it's hard or easy. Apparently there is usually only one seeker and lots of hiders, but today we play the other way round: Matteo and Etienne stand with their backs to me, covering their eyes with their hands and counting rather quickly to a hundred.

I take Astra by the scruff of the neck and clamber beneath the cover of the rowing boat as quietly as I can. It's such an obvious hiding place that I'm hoping they won't find me here. I realise that I am holding my breath and holding on to Astra far too tightly. I try to relax and enjoy the cool, damp air that is a welcome relief after the relentless heat of the southern European sun.

The bottom of the rowing boat has small pools of water in it and, because of the three wooden seats placed at the front (where Matteo always sits), the middle (Etienne's place) and the back (my place, it seems), I can't get comfortable. I can't believe I fell asleep here after chasing Astra up the gangplank!

Five. Four. Three. Two. One!

'Coming to get you, ready or not!' shouts Matteo gleefully.

Am I ready? Or not? I don't know.

I hold my breath. The sound of bare feet on the deck,

as they run in opposite directions to find me. Disturbed by the noise, Astra jumps off my chest and lands in a pool of stagnant water. She yowls loudly.

'Ha!' says Matteo, tearing back the cover. 'Etienne! I found her in the row boat. It's your turn.'

Etienne appears behind Matteo, peeping over his shoulder and grinning.

Matteo and I count, our eyes covered. On ten, I open my eyes and see Astra stretching her back legs one at a time, as though she has just done a lot of strenuous exercise. She jumps on to the top of the rowing boat and reclines on the hot cover on her back, her front and back legs lengthened.

'Come on,' says Matteo. We set off to search for Etienne.

He's not in the slop room, where the crew's clothing is traditionally kept (it has a few spare sailor's caps and jackets, but not much else). He's not in the coalhole, alongside the coal and wood. He's not snoozing in a hammock in the sick bay. He's not in the bread room. We tentatively knock on Claude's door, but the cabin is empty. He's not in Matteo's cabin, nor mine.

We peer up at the mainsail, but he's not even

cheekily hanging out up there.

He is nowhere to be found.

Matteo looks at me. He looks worried. He grabs the telescope, which is dangling from a nail by the prow of the ship, and runs from one end of the ship to the other, from port to starboard, looking out to sea. I run to the prow of the ship and look into the sea. *Surely he can swim? Surely I would be able to see him?* The waves are gentle and the wind has dropped to the extent that we are drifting rather than racing towards Sicily.

'Etienne!' I shout.

Several seagulls shriek in response. A flock of sand martins flies past, allowing the wind to carry their dark brown and white bodies northwards. They are the smallest European hirundines – the group name for martins and swallows – and they travel from Africa to Europe in the summer and return all the way to Africa for the winter. I thought our voyage to Sicily was long, but it's nothing compared to these small birds. Nature always puts everything in perspective.

The sun is so dazzling that tiny dots dance in front of my eyes. I blink hard and see something out of the corner of my eye. A ship, more or less the same size as *Anthos*, is bearing down on us.

I try to shout Matteo's name, but my tongue is as heavy as a stone at the bottom of my mouth. I try to turn my head, to wave my arms, but it's as though my body has been set in resin, like a fossil. I look for Otis and his father. I look for the mass of black curls.

But there's no one on the ship. Which means . . . no one is sailing the ship.

'Nico!' shouts Matteo from the other end of the ship. 'I found Etienne! He had locked himself in the chain locker room!'

I turn to see Matteo leading Etienne across the deck, his hand firmly placed on his friend's shoulder as though he doesn't want to let go of him any time soon. I'm about to tell them about the mysterious ship, but when I turn, it's vanished, like a strange dream.

15

3 May 1832

Late in the afternoon, I water the salad leaves, radishes and red peppers and decide they are ready to harvest. I fill a bucket with the radish leaves, the perfect pink and white spheres and the misshapen peppers and take them to the galley. It is too early for supper, but everyone is already sitting there, even Aunt Ruth. They look at me as I proudly empty the bucket on to the table.

'I have been growing these secretly,' I say. 'To surprise you all.'

'We know,' says everyone around the table in unison.

'There are very few
secrets on this ship,'
says Matteo,
raising an eyebrow
in my direction.

'Oh,' I say, slumping down in my seat, deflated.

'Thank you, Nico,' says Claude, reaching for a radish. 'Back in France we would dip these into butter and then salt. *Magnifique!*'

Aunt Ruth puts a hand on my arm. 'Yes, thank you, Nico. Your thoughtfulness is appreciated. We won't have to worry about getting scurvy now!'

'Why is everyone here?' I ask.

Etienne grabs a radish and pops it into his mouth. His eyes widen. 'I had forgotten how peppery they are!'

'We are here to discuss the next stage of our journey,' says the captain, eyeing a red pepper. 'I thought you might like to know more about the history of Sicily in general and Palermo in particular. And then we can discuss some specific plans for the moment we reach Palermo.'

'Yes please!' I say, my mood immediately brightening.

'Well, Palermo is a city informed by many cultures. A city that had been invaded by – in no particular order – the Normans, the Greeks, the Spaniards, the Romans and the Arabs. And some others you might not be so familiar with: the Phoenicians, who occupied a narrow piece of land along the coast of Syria, Lebanon and northern Israel; the Carthaginians, who were early Phoenicians, and the Vandals – a Germanic people with their own pirate fleets!'

He tugs at his beard. 'Sicily has so many stories. As I have said before, it really is a land of magic and myth . . .'

'It's also a land of recorded history and true events,' says Aunt, winking at the captain. I thought she was serious pretty much all the time, but evidently not.

The captain raises his eyes to heaven: this is clearly an ongoing argument about fact versus fiction, about myth versus reality. It's one they also clearly have unexpected fun with.

'On the east coast of Sicily,' continues the captain, 'Odysseus and his men were imprisoned in a cave by the Cyclops, Polyphemus. They blinded the monster, then escaped by clinging to the bellies of his sheep. To a certain extent, I agree with Dr Hamilton: there are so many apocryphal stories that it's impossible to know if any or all are true. Take Archimedes, the Sicilian-Greek mathematician. Did he really defend Syracuse from Roman ships using mirrors? Did he really invent the Claw of Archimedes?'

I remember reading about the Claw of Archimedes – a large crane with a grappling hook that could be angled until it caught the ship's prow and then toppled it over – but I have no memory of the story being set in Sicily.

'Tell us more, Papà,' says Matteo. He looks proud. I am not surprised; this is his heritage, his land. I feel envious; England is so dull in comparison.

'I think it's time for Dr Hamilton to speak,' says the captain.

Aunt Ruth wipes her huge glasses on her grey shirt. 'Once we moor at the harbour in Palermo, I will stay aboard *Anthos*, as will Etienne, Claude and the captain. I know the captain and Matteo will be impatient to see their family, but I'm afraid that work must come first. Time is not on our side. As each day passes, I am increasingly anxious. I am so close to something wonderful, something that could benefit all of mankind – but I'm not quite there yet. If the other scientists or their men get there before me, I am afraid it will not be in the interest of the human race, but in the interest only of profit. Many of my peers see financial reward as the sole impetus for hard work . . .'

'Dr Hamilton,' I say. 'The plan.'

'Oh yes, I was rather going off topic, wasn't I? Well.

First of all, I am still not one hundred per cent convinced that the Tree of Hope ever existed. Which of course means there will be no fossilised seeds to find.'

'We have to believe the Tree existed,' I say firmly. 'We've come too far not to believe.'

Aunt ignores me and carries on talking, as slowly as if English were a language she had just started learning. 'However, if the captain's *nonna* is right and the tree really *did* exist at some time in the distant past and there *are* fossilised seeds . . .'

'And where do you think they will be, Dr Hamilton?' I ask, knowing the answer but want to hear her talk through her thoughts again.

'Well, they can only really be in the botanical gardens, just as the captain's *nonna* thought.'

'Agreed!' says the captain. 'The *giardino botanico* is indeed the best bet.'

'Those who work in the garden are very serious about

the cultivation of medicinal plants, which is always something to celebrate,' says Aunt. 'One day, when the importance of conserving seeds is fully understood, I believe that Palermo's botanical garden will become an important destination.'

'Can we go to the *giardino* . . . the botanical garden as soon as we arrive in Palermo?' I ask eagerly.

'You and Matteo can,' says the captain.

'What about me?' asks Etienne, pouting.

'You are strong,' says the Claude. 'You need to guard the ship with us.'

Etienne's pout shifts into a smile; he appears to be satisfied with this answer.

'And, as I said earlier, I have work to be getting on with,' says Aunt. 'The captain tells me the gardens are less than half an hour by foot from the harbour. Matteo speaks pretty good Italian, I believe, should you get lost. The challenge will be this: you have to find the fossilised seeds, should they exist, before nightfall. Remember, Mr King has Nico's notebook; it will lead him straight to the garden. Unless he's taken a wrong turn of course – he might be in America for all we know.'

Now that Aunt is talking about facts and plans, she is precise and eloquent; it is the talk of myths that makes her hesitate. I want to be brilliant at science like her, but I want to believe in magic sometimes too.

Aunt stands. 'I am going to do some more work before supper,' she says. 'Nico, can I have a word with you in my cabin?'

I follow her down the salt-stained stairs to her cabin, wondering what she is going to say. That I am not up to it? That I have led them all on a wild goose chase?

She stands in the doorway of her cabin and puts her hand on my shoulder. 'I will be taking supper in my cabin tonight so I will see you when you are back from your trip. And, Nico – *stammi bene*. Italian for "take care", I believe. I don't want to lose the best assistant I've ever had.'

I look at her, my mouth hanging wide open.

'Don't look so surprised,' she says. 'I am only tough on you because I have extremely high expectations of you.'

'Thank you,' is all I can think of saying; but, as I return to the galley to help prepare supper, my heart is singing.

*

The sky is midnight blue. So blue, it's almost black. The stars are winking at us as we lie on our backs, side by side, in the middle of the deck. Matteo, me, Etienne. Astra sits on my stomach, but when I start to fidget, she goes and curls up inside the small gap between Etienne's arm and his chest. He moves the telescope to the other side of his body so that she has more room if she needs it.

'Do you know . . .' I say.

Matteo and Etienne burst out laughing.

'I'm not showing off!' I say, smiling.

'Go on,' says Etienne. 'Surprise us.'

'Most stars are between one and ten billion years old. The most common stars are red dwarf stars, which are half the size of the sun; they can live as long as 100 billion years. Stars are all sorts of different colours, depending how hot they are. Blue is the hottest, followed by white, then yellow and finally red. The light from the stars takes millions of years to reach Earth – so, lying here, we're actually looking back in time.'

'You mean . . .' says Etienne. 'Stars are like fossils?'

'Exactly,' I say. 'I would love to meet a real-life astronomer and find out what they know about ancient stars. Maybe one day.'

'Hey, Astra, did you know your name is an anagram of "a star"?' asks Etienne, rubbing her chin till her purring is so loud it almost drowns out his words.

I didn't know Etienne liked cats so much. Or that they liked him so much in return. *Maybe she likes him more than me?* No, that's ridiculous.

I look up at the dome of sky and stars and then look at Etienne and Matteo. They are truly great friends. Friends I feel safe sharing anything with.

'Once, when I was sent to my room by Mother and Father for speaking out of turn, I tried to learn the Latin names of plants to distract me from crying. I found myself learning some phrases too. Phrases that might help me when I was feeling a bit . . . lost. The only one I remembered was *per aspera ad astra*. "*Aspera*" is hardship and "*astra*" is star. So it means "through hardship to the stars".'

'So you've called your cat "stars"?' asks Etienne.

'Oh gosh!' I say. 'I think she should really be called "*astrum*" as that refers to a single star, but it's not such a catchy name.'

'True,' says Etienne, gently stroking the cat.

'I don't think Astra or Astrum cares what you call her as long as she's fed. Anyway, wouldn't it be easier to remember "achieve the impossible" rather than something as boring as "through hardship to the stars"?' says Matteo, laughing. 'But I'm sorry you were upset.'

'Are you mocking me?' I ask, prodding him in the side.

'It would be a shame not to,' he says. 'It's my turn to show off. See that semi-circle of white up there in the sky?

It's appears to grow bigger and then shrinks in size, otherwise known as waxing and waning . . .'

'Very funny, Matteo,' says Etienne. 'We all know about the moon!'

We laugh and joke and Matteo tells us about orange-red Mars, bright white Jupiter and golden-yellow Saturn. He points out Ursa Major and Ursa Minor, Big and Little Bear, and the eerie glow of the billions of stars that make up the Milky Way.

And then we lie in silence for a long time, looking up at the vast universe and feeling very small, but very alive.

When clouds obscure the moon, I shiver.

'I'm going to my hammock,' I say, picking Astra up and draping her sleepy body over my shoulder. '*Sogni d'oro.*'

'Sweet dreams to you too,' says Matteo.

'*Per aspera ad astra,*' says Etienne, his voice heavy with sleep.

16

I twist and turn in my hammock. My mind is whirring and hissing and humming.

I know that this will be one of those nights when I just can't get to sleep and the harder I try, the less sleepy I will become. Astra is lying on her side in front of the fire, her front paws crossed over each other. I kneel beside her, stroke her back softly and listen to her contented purr.

At home, I used to get out of bed on such nights and wander silently around the house, sometimes walking barefoot on the damp grass in the garden. I would stare up at the stars and wonder who else might be looking at the same stars at exactly the same time. Perhaps a girl my age in France. Or Italy. Or Norway. I used to think a kid in America might be looking at the same stars, but then I read that the time in America is different and it would still be daytime there.

Perhaps Matteo and Etienne will still be out there, staring into space. I shut the cabin door quietly behind me and pad across the decking. There they are, exactly as I left them, their bodies as still as stone.

'Matteo!' I whisper.

He doesn't move.

'Etienne!'

His eyes are shut, his arms neatly by his side.

Surely I haven't been gone long enough for anything bad to happen to them? Surely the Kings didn't sneak on board while I was gone . . .

I crouch down over Matteo and put my hand in

front of his nose, to see if I can feel his breath. But I wobble and end up tilting forward and clamping my hand over his mouth. His eyes open and he stares at me in shock.

I whip my hand away and wipe it on my trousers. 'Sorry! I couldn't sleep . . . I thought you were—'

'What's going on?' asks Etienne, jumping to his feet, his fists raised.

'Nico thought we were dead!' says Matteo, laughing so hard his dimple seems to expand across his cheek.

'It's not funny,' I say, hugging my arms around myself. 'I was scared.'

Etienne looks serious. 'Who's lookout?'

'You,' says Matteo. 'Only you fell asleep and now Otis King is probably asleep and snoring in your hammock.'

'Have you lost your mind?' asks Etienne, picking up the telescope. 'This isn't a time for jokes. Or for taking risks by leaving the ship defenceless. We are so close to Sicily now . . .'

Matteo stands up, rubbing his eyes. 'I'd say we've got no evidence of anyone chasing after us.'

What if the ship I saw when we were playing hide and seek was real? Should I tell them?

'Well, you can't be sure of anything,' says Etienne, striding off to the stern without looking back. The moment is gone.

My eyes sting. I am suddenly overwhelmed with exhaustion and turn to head back to my cabin.

Matteo hurries behind me. 'Nico, wait. If you can't sleep, I could take the other hammock in your cabin and we could talk. Talking always helps. Papà tells me stories about Sicily when I can't sleep and the next thing I know, it's morning.'

'Fine,' I say, my voice shrill.

'I didn't mean to laugh at you,' says Matteo, putting

an arm around me. 'It was just a shock to wake up with your hand over my mouth and realise that you thought we were both corpses.'

Sulking never got me anywhere, I think. *You have a friend. Don't lose him.*

'Sorry I shocked you,' I say.

'I'll get over it,' he says. 'You go ahead. I'll make some tea and bring it to the cabin to warm us up.'

*

The air in the cabin is slightly damp. I add a few extra pieces of wood to the stove and the walls take on an orange hue as the flames grow.

'What shall we talk about?' asks Matteo, putting his tea on the floor and stretching his long legs right to the end of the spare hammock and pulling the blankets up to his chin.

'What are you most scared of?' I ask, blowing on the hot drink and wondering if I have to pretend to like it.

I expect him to pause, to think about an answer, but
he barely hesitates. 'Father dying. Catastrophic storms.
Not having enough food to eat. Spiders. You?'

I prop myself on a pile of blankets so I can see Matteo
clearly. 'Spiders! They are more likely to be scared of *you*.
I'm scared of . . .' I suddenly feel vulnerable, but it's only
fair to share back. 'I'm scared of forgetting everything I
know and never owning another book again and not
being able to keep secrets.'

'What sort of secrets?' asks Matteo.

Dr Hamilton is my aunt . . .

'I can't tell you about my secrets for obvious reasons.'

He laughs. 'Do you think it's OK to keep secrets?'

'If you are protecting people, maybe. If you aren't hurting anyone and no one needs to know . . .'

'What else are you scared of?' asks Matteo, leaning over and picking up his tea. He tips it all into his mouth in one go, as though it's a cold drink.

'Not being allowed to study science at university. Not being allowed to become a scientist one day.' I pause and sip the tea. *Disgusting.* 'Being alone.'

'You aren't alone, Nico,' he says, turning to me. 'You have friends. And friends tell each other things. My mother was fascinated by science. She was teaching herself natural history when she became pregnant with me. She wanted to find a way of studying creatures that live in the ocean. My father was saving up to buy his own ship so that she could do her research while he sailed the ship and looked after me. But it never happened . . .'

He is showing me his heart.

I look at his face, glowing in the light from the stove. His eyes are wet with tears, but he doesn't try to brush them away.

'Is that why your father is captain of *Anthos*?' I ask gently. 'Because he knows what incredible work scientists do?'

Matteo nods. 'He wants to help Dr Hamilton fulfil his research. He doesn't make a big song and dance about it. He just wants to make the journey safely, without the scientists in London managing to get hold of Dr Hamilton's life's work.'

'I didn't know fathers could be good men until I met yours,' I say. I want to ask more about his mother, but it's up to him to tell me about her, when he is ready. If he is ever ready.

He doesn't say anything and, when I look across the

cabin, his eyes are closed. He is smiling and I'm not sure if you can smile in your sleep.

'When I ran away from home for the day, part of me wanted Mother and Father to stop me. I even slammed the front door. I waited at the end of the road. But no one came.' The fire crackles softly. 'You are like the brother I always wanted.'

'And you are the sister I never knew I wanted,' says Matteo groggily.

'With your land legs and my sea legs, we can do anything,' I say.

'We can achieve the impossible,' he says, without opening his eyes.

*

The botanical garden is empty: no plants, no locked room, no people. Just a cavernous building with cracked walls and holes in the roof. A ship is sailing towards Anthos, faster and faster. It's too late to tack left or right. It's getting closer and closer. Someone is in my room again, emptying my bag on to the floor. Tucking Astra under their arm, taking her away from me —

I sit up in my hammock. My armpits are drenched. Astra doesn't seem to mind; she simply purrs when I move.

'Matteo,' I whisper.

He groans and turns to me. The amber lights of the fire show his face enough for me to see the criss-cross pattern of the hammock imprinted on his face – he forgot to put a blanket beneath his head.

'Are you OK?' he asks.

I tell him about my dream – my nightmare. 'I was sure that someone was in the cabin,' I say. 'And – I saw a ship when we were playing hide and seek. Or I thought I did. The sun was so bright. A ghost ship, with no one on it. I don't know any more what is real and what is a dream.'

'I don't think you saw a ship,' he says gently. 'And I

don't think anyone has come into your cabin at night. But I can only say "I don't *think*". I can't be sure. Sometimes you can't be sure about things. We don't know if the Tree of Hope existed. We are going to try to find out, but we may never know.'

My heart lurches. 'Don't say that. We *have* to find the fossilised seeds. We *have* to believe.'

He continues, sounding terribly grown-up. 'And I *do* believe, but I'm not going to lie and say that I'm 100 per cent sure our trip to the *giardino botanico* will be successful.'

Our hammocks suddenly swing violently from side to side.

Matteo sits up. 'The wind has picked up. It must be another storm.'

'Does that mean we must sail into the waves full on?'

He frowns at me.

'You told me that on my first day,' I say. 'When you said I didn't know a thing about ships.'

251

The boat tilts to one side and Astra slides across the floor, coming to a halt beneath my hammock.

Matteo leaps out of the hammock and is out of the door before I can even sit up.

Astra's huge green eyes peer out at me from beneath the hammock.

I pull on my boots and then the raincoat, taking forever to button it up with my shaking hands. All I see outside the cabin is darkness. I grab hold of a rail as the ship leans heavily first to port and then to starboard. The captain is shouting instructions, but all I can hear are distant sounds, not the actual words.

I know by now that if the ship leans too far, it will capsize. And then it will sink.

As soon as my eyes adjust, I see big, black waves attacking us at speed, one after the other.

I run across the deck, into the fierce wind, and find Matteo and Etienne trying to secure the mainsail, which has already sustained what looks like serious damage.

'Can I help?' I shout, as water sloshes up the side of the ship and drenches me in thick spray. There's no reply.

During the first storm – a lifetime ago, surely? – I was wondering if I dare tuck my dress into my knickers. Now I want to stop the ship from descending silently to the bottom of the sea.

'Nico!' I turn to see the captain, his beard glistening with beads of seawater in the pale light of the moon. 'Claude is at the helm, guiding *Anthos* as best he can. Help him. Before it's too late.'

I sprint, slide, skid and tumble across the deck, praying that a greedy wave won't seize me and sling me into the sea. Clouds cover the moon and the sky is as black as ink. I'm already soaked through.

Claude stands on the small wooden platform beneath the wheel, his navy shirt billowing out behind him. He holds on to the small mahogany handles so tightly that his knuckles have turned white. His cap is tucked into the waist of his trousers and his hair is being blown upwards by the wind. He is sailing into the sea like one of the carved wooden figureheads that I've read about; he looks as if he can somehow offer the same power and protection.

'How can I help?' I yell above the wind.

'Stand on the wooden platform and hold tight!'

I do as he says and slip into the space between Claude and the wheel. He takes my hands and places them firmly on the handles – if the wheel were a clock, my left hand would be at ten and my right at two. He stands on the other side of the wheel, facing me, and puts his hands at nine and three.

The wheel turns violently to the left and, for a moment, it feels as though my whole body is going to fly through the air, following the trajectory of the wheel.

'Hold tight!' shouts Claude again.

I think of Astra, sliding across the floor in our cabin.

I think of Matteo and Etienne, trying to rescue the mainsail.

I think of Dr Hamilton, alone in her cabin, so close to achieving a scientific breakthrough which could change the way we live.

I hold on to the handles with every last drop of strength in my body. I help Claude twist the wheel back to the right, **pushing, pushing, pushing**. We stand as steadily as statues, me at ten and two, Claude at nine and three. We barely dare to breathe.

My body is about to break. I have no strength left. I am close to tears of pure frustration. I want to wipe the rain from my eyelashes, but I dare not take my hands off the wheel, so I shake my head until I can see again. I think of the flock of sand martins, so tiny and brave, travelling thousands of miles across land and sea. They make it because they aren't alone.

Beyond Claude, through the driving rain and the

vicious wind, I see a shape. I blink hard. The moon forces
its way through the clouds. The prow of a ship looms in
the darkness. Claude's eyes squint in concentration. I
squint into the gloom. I cannot see the ship, but there
is . . . a figurehead. Carved out of wood. A woman. I
think. Yes, a woman. A woman with a sword through her
neck. I shake the rain away again.

'Santa Lucia?' I whisper.

A vast cloud shrouds the moon once more and I can see nothing but darkness behind Claude. Nothing at all.

And then the wheel stops battling with us, as though it's suddenly given up.

'It's over,' says Claude.

'Over?' I ask, suddenly feeling faint.

'The storm. It's gone to pick on another ship.' Claude wipes his forearm across his brow. 'You can let go now. Thank you, Nico.'

My palms are covered in tiny blisters. My shoulders ache. I can barely believe we managed to hold on to the wheel.

Behind Claude, to the east, the sea is still black, but the sky is midnight blue once more and on the distant horizon is a thin strip of orange-yellow light.

'Look!' I say to Claude, pointing over his shoulder.

'Ah yes,' he says, twisting around to take in the view.

'It is always darkest before dawn.'

I return to my cabin, grateful for the calm that follows a storm, and fall almost immediately into a dreamless sleep.

17

10 May 1832

Palermo, at last. The port is packed with every type of ship and sailing boat you could imagine, some newly painted in blue, orange or red, others so rusty that they look as though they might crumble if you tapped them lightly. Most of the ships are much bigger and sturdier than *Anthos* and look ready for battle, while some of the fishing boats look too flimsy to be able to take on wild seas. *Anthos*, berthed in a shaded corner of the harbour at the end of a long wooden walkway, seemed to breathe a sigh of relief when the captain dropped anchor, as though

she didn't quite believe we'd make it.

It is everything I dreamed of and more. Matteo and I stand on the dock with our backs to the port and stare at the city untangling in front of us. Here we finally find ourselves, in the land of magic and myth. We are going to save the world with the Tree of Hope seeds. I can feel it in my bones.

Even though it is early, barely an hour past dawn, the sea shimmers with heat and the port swarms with people. There are no snowy clouds of flour dust here, no children begging – at least not that I can see. Instead the locals dash past, their arms laden with fresh bread and dazzling orange and yellow fruits that I have never seen before, or even read about – oranges and lemons, says Matteo, leaning heavily against a wall. His legs are still wobbly and we must wait until he has acclimatised to the stillness of the ground. Beads of sweat gather on his forehead and I am glad to be wearing my summer dress for the first time since I became an accidental stowaway.

'I am starving,' I say, staring at someone dashing by with yet another loaf of warm bread, coated in tiny white sesame seeds.

'You're in luck then,' he says, reaching in his pocket and pulling out a handful of large notes. 'Father says this should be enough to buy everyone on Anthos some *arancini*.'

'Some . . . what did you say?'

'A-rrrrr-an-chee-nee,' he says slowly. 'Do you remember father talking about the feast of Santa Lucia? Well, as well as eating *cuccìa*, we also eat *arancini* – which is Italian for "little oranges", due to their shape. But most importantly they taste delicious: if you haven't eaten deep-fried balls of rice filled with things like meat, mozzarella and peas, then you haven't lived!'

'But it's not December, it's July. I remember the captain saying that the feast of Santa Lucia is on the thirteenth of December.'

'We don't only eat *arancini* on that particular day,' says Matteo, rolling his eyes, and doing little to hide his impatience. I know he is at his worst when he's tired and hungry, but sometimes I wish he could remember to be kind. He pushes himself away from the wall and strides into the crowd.

'Wait,' I shout.

He is swallowed up by the locals and I can only keep track of him by his ears, which jut out like sails. It occurs to me that his mother never had the chance to hold him upside down by his ears; perhaps his father did.

Without turning round, Matteo thrusts a hand behind him and I grab it gratefully, holding on as tightly as I can. We thread our way through the crowd until we reach a man selling fresh *arancini* from a small wooden stall. The smell of rice and saffron fills the air. Even with an abundance of radishes and peppers and salad leaves, it's so long since we ate hot, fresh food that I wish we had enough money to buy ten each.

'*Sei arancini*,' says Matteo confidently, but holds up six fingers just in case. The man, with deep-set eyes and sunken cheeks, smiles and nods. He wraps six crispy *arancini* balls in a sheet of paper, pops them in a brown

bag and accepts more than half the notes in return.

Matteo gives me one of the *arancini* and we bite into them greedily, squealing at the unexpected heat held in the centre of the ball and the sensation of the cheese melting on our tongues.

Afterwards, we cool our mouths with cups of lemon *granita*, our faces contorting at the sour tang of this wondrous new fruit.

'My brain hurts,' I say.

'That will be the ice in the *granita*,' says Matteo, laughing.

Behind him, in amongst the throng of people, I see a mass of curly black hair and a flash of blue and gold.

'Nico? Your face looks odd. Is it the *granita*?'

I shake my head, staring over his shoulder. He turns and scans the crowd.

'Did you see something?' he asks.

Not something. Someone.

But I can't be sure – I still don't even know if the ghost ship I saw was real – and I don't want Matteo to think I'm daydreaming or imagining things again, so I shake my head. 'It's nothing. Let's take the *arancini* back to the ship before they go cold.'

*

We promised the captain we'd be quick, but on the way back Matteo is distracted by a bakery whose window display is full of *cannoli* – crispy pastry shells stuffed with sweet white ricotta – that we can't afford. In the distance, church bells chime, as though to remind us that we haven't got time to be standing around.

'Let's go,' I say, pulling him away from the shop window by his elbow. He shakes himself free and walks ahead of me again: this is his island and it is his job to show me the way back to the ship.

As soon as we return to the port, I see that something is wrong. The captain is standing on the narrow wooden walkway that leads to *Anthos*. His face is ashen and his eyes dart left and right as he scans the crowd.

When he sees us he beckons us on to the ship.

'Papà, what's wrong?' Matteo asks.

'I don't want to talk here,' says the captain. 'Follow me to the sick bay.'

Matteo and I follow him along the deck in single file, as though in a funeral procession, the captain at the front, then Matteo, clutching the bag of warm *arancini* to his chest, and finally me. The smell of the *arancini* turns my stomach.

'In here,' says the captain, almost pushing Matteo and I into the sick bay. Claude is perched on the edge of the old, scratched wooden table, his face pale and his eyes wide.

The captain shuts the door behind him. Matteo and I balance on the edge of adjacent hammocks.

'It's terrible news,' says Claude, pushing up his hair. 'Just terrible.'

The captain stands in the middle of the small room. 'Etienne and Astra are missing,' he says. 'We think Otis King and his father have taken them. Though goodness knows how – Etienne is such a strong boy.'

'How do you know the Pirate Kings have taken them?' I ask slowly. 'What if Etienne decided to take Astra for a walk? Or to get some special Italian cat food in Palermo?' I know it's extremely unlikely, but I'm trying to think of anything to block out the truth.

Matteo stands. 'You mean . . . you mean that Etienne and Astra have been kidnapped?'

The captain and Claude nod gravely.

'It's my fault,' I say. 'I made everyone come here.'

'If it's anyone's fault, it's the scientists in London,' says the captain.

'I'm going back on deck,' says Claude, jumping to his feet. 'I can't stay here and do nothing. I'll ask passers-by if they saw anything . . .'

The captain nods in agreement and Claude rushes out. The captain continues. 'Claude and I are pretty sure that Otis and his father Herman will only release Etienne and the cat if we give them something in return. Something that we can't give them.'

'The fossilised seeds?' I ask.

He nods.

'But we haven't even been to the botanical garden yet,' I say, doing my best to sound calm as my heart thuds in my chest and whooshes in my ears.

'Come right now!' Claude appears at the door of the sick bay.

The captain is up and out of the sick bay in a flash. Matteo and I scramble out of our hammocks and follow, Matteo still clutching his cooling bag of *arancini*.

Claude and the captain are standing on the deck, heads bent over something.

'Please,' I say. 'Tell us what is going on.'

Claude hands me a piece of paper. 'I just found this in the middle of the deck, weighed down by a stone.'

WE HAVE YOUR BOY + CAT. WE WILL HARM BOTH UNLESS YOU HAND OVER THE FOSSILISED SEEDS FROM THE BOTANICAL GARDEN. THE BOY AND GIRL MUST COME TO FORT ARENELLA BEFORE DUSK. IN THE ROWING BOAT. NO ADULTS. YOURS. OTIS KING.

My stomach flips. My body feels as though it could drift away, over the sea and into nothingness.

'We *have* to inform Dr Hamilton at once,' says Claude.

'I agree,' says the captain, tugging at his beard again. 'We can't let you go to the *giardino botanico* in case this is some kind of trick.'

'You have to let us go,' I say, taking Matteo's hand.

'And we will make sure we have something to give to the Kings,' says Matteo, gripping my hand as firmly as he might were he dangling from the side of *Anthos*, about to fall into the sea. He holds out the paper bag. 'We will bring our friends back, Papà. Don't let the *arancini* go cold.'

18

Palermo is thick with heat and people. We pass churches guarded by marble statues and narrow alleyways dominated by rusty iron balconies overflowing with pink and red geraniums. Clean sheets strung between the balconies drift in the warm breeze. We step around skinny stray cats begging for morsels of food that I would usually stop to stroke. There is no time for cats or *cannoli*, no time for anything except finding the fossilised seeds that might not even exist.

I stop and turn around as often as I dare, without

Matteo noticing. No one appears to be following, not that I can see.

The entrance to the botanical garden is flanked by stone sphinxes. They have the body of a lion with the wings of an eagle and the head of a human. Their eyes peer at us suspiciously; *who are you and what do you want?*

This morning I'd have thought: *To feed the world with the Tree of Hope seeds.* Now I simply think: *To save our friend and my cat. Please.*

Matteo pauses by one sphinx and taps its left paw. 'For luck,' he says. 'My father told me about it.' I see that the paw has been worn smooth from being touched so many times.

We step through the gates. The first thing I notice is the dozens of imposing palm trees, with tall thin trunks crowned with green feathery leaves, that shade us from the soaring heat. Stone fountains shoot out cool water that I would like to sit in right now if we weren't in such a rush. A girl with curly hair about my age sits in the shade underneath one of them, her face buried in a book. *I wish I could be her*, I think, *without a care in the world*. Suddenly my boring life back home doesn't seem so bad. I wanted an adventure, but I didn't count on a kidnapping.

We walk quickly through the hot house, which is oddly silent and airless, but smells sweet and earthy. We push past the vast green leaves of plants with bright orange flowers, all reaching for the sun, all competing for attention, and I wish we had time to stop and read about their stories. Where are they from? Why do they love the humidity so much?

The other end of the hot house opens out on to a deliciously cool and dark hallway that is lined with a series of doors. Matteo stops in front of one that says: *SOLO IL PERSONALE* and another that says *INGRESSO VIETATO*.

273

'What do those signs mean?' I ask Matteo.

'STAFF ONLY and DO NOT ENTER,' whispers Matteo. 'I'm pretty sure, anyway.'

'Do you think we should risk going into the DO NOT ENTER room?' I whisper back. 'Maybe the seed fossils are in there.'

'Not sure. Oh hang on, it must be this one!' He stops by a door that says ANCIENT RELICS in English. The room with the locked door! It really exists. There is a glimmer of hope.

'Try the handle,' I whisper, looking up and down the corridor. It's still empty.

Matteo twists the handle this way and that. The door doesn't move.

'It's locked, just as Papà's *nonna* thought.'

I remember how hard it was to open my cabin door in the storm. 'Maybe it's just stuck,' I say. I square up to the door. I turn the handle and push the door with my shoulder. Once, twice. Third time lucky! The door swings open and I tumble into a dark, dusty and slightly damp room.

It smells of history.

'I can't see a thing,' I whisper.

'Your eyes will adjust,' says Matteo.

'*Buongiorno*,' says a deep voice.

My heart quickens. There's someone in here!

A pause before the man's voice fills the room again. 'Sicilian? English?'

'Sicilian,' says Matteo proudly, in the deepest voice he can manage.

'English,' I say, quietly.

I squint into the darkness. I can just about make out a shape in the far corner of the room.

There is the loud sound of wood hitting stone and suddenly the room is filled with light. A young man, who must only be about sixteen years old, stands by a window – he has flung open the wooden shutters against the thick stone wall.

The room, previously hidden from sight, reveals itself. It is packed full of display cases showing off fossils and sketches and ancient books. If only Aunt Ruth could be here!

'I am Vincenzo Piazzi,' says the boy. He takes off his dark blue hat and gives a small bow. He is dressed in the most beautiful clothes: dark blue trousers, brown leather shoes that look virtually unworn, a spotless white shirt and, despite the heat, a blue jacket a shade lighter than the trousers. He looks as though he hasn't worked a day in his life.

'Matteo D'Angelo,' says Matteo, extending his hand.

'I am Nico Cloud,' I say, doing the same. Vincenzo's hand is as soft as a baby's – like mine used to be before I was put to work on *Anthos*.

'As in Nicoletta?' asks Vincenzo.

'As in Nico,' I say, smiling. *Can we trust this man?*

'Very well, Nico,' he says. 'This room isn't open for the public, I'm afraid. I had just turned the lights off and shut the shutters when you barged your way in. Let me show you the way out.'

He starts to walk towards the door.

'Wait,' says Matteo. 'My papà's *nonna* told us about this room. We came here by ship this morning to find it.'

Vincenzo stops. 'I have heard about a boat that arrived in the port last night that has pirates on board,' he says slowly.

I stare at Matteo and he stares back. 'We are most certainly not pirates,' says Matteo. 'In fact, we despise them!'

Vincenzo steps closer to Matteo. 'I don't suppose you are related to Tommaso D'Angelo, the great sea captain?'

'Yes!' Matteo says, his dimple expanding across his cheek.

'I am sorry for your loss,' says Vincenzo.

'You know about my *mamma*?' says Matteo, his eyes filling with water.

Vincenzo nods. 'My *nonna* Maria grew up alongside your *nonna* Lydia,' he says. 'Lydia's heart was broken when Tommaso sent news of his wife's death in childbirth.'

'Is *nonna* Lydia . . .'

Vincenzo nods. 'She's very much alive, my friend. Her husband – your grandfather – passed away some time ago. *Nonna* Lydia lives in the same village as my *nonna* Maria, in the shadows of Mount Etna. I can take you to her – if you have time?'

Matteo nods furiously. 'I can't believe you know my family!'

Vincenzo laughs. 'Sicily is not that small, but everybody has heard of Tommaso D'Angelo. Not only because he's a great sea captain, but because he works for a great, but very mysterious, scientist. Dr Hamilton, I think his name is.'

I have to stop myself from shouting out, *that's my aunt!*

There's a clattering in the corridor and my heart quickens. *Has Otis followed us?* I turn quickly and a woman walks past, holding a broken plant pot in one hand and a green plant with a bright orange flower in the other. Luckily, she is too flustered to pay us any attention.

We have to be able to trust this man in his smart clothes. He's our only hope. 'Vincenzo,' I say, lowering my voice just in case anyone else is listening. 'What do you know about the Tree of Hope?'

Vincenzo smiles. 'I think it is time for you to meet *il principe.*'

19

Vincenzo's horse and cart is in a shady spot outside the gardens, watched over by a young boy who looks no older than seven.

'This is us,' he says, handing a few notes to the boy. 'You two sit at the back. Here, put these on.'

He hands us each a straw hat and climbs on to the driver's seat. We do as we are told and sit in silence, feeling a bit daft in the wide-brimmed hats, but very glad for the protection from the brutally hot sun. We bump through dusty streets that are now eerily quiet.

Peeling wooden shutters are shut against the sun, but the windows behind them are open and there's the faint chink of cutlery on china and the most divine aromas drift out into the street, making me salivate. The Italians really do take their food seriously, and I can't say I blame them if it smells that good.

The narrow coastal road is spectacular. Vincenzo, who says *buongiorno* to every single cart that passes, doesn't even bother looking out at the turquoise ocean, but Matteo and I are transfixed by its almost unreal colour. The sides of the endlessly twisting road are carpeted in vibrant blue, white, orange and red wild flowers. I wish I could stop, just for a moment, to pick some. I could dry the seeds and grow them myself on *Anthos*.

'*Siamo arrivati*!' announces Vincenzo. 'We are here!'

We stop at a wrought iron gate. He hops off the cart to open it, leads the horse through, then closes it behind us. He pats the horse, hops back on and drives us up a long, cobbled driveway and into a large courtyard, packed so tightly with trees and shrubs and flowers that there is not much room to park the horse and cart.

We stumble off the cart, feeling a little sick from all the twists and turns of the coastal road that brought us here. Matteo holds on to the cart for a moment to steady himself.

'*Benvenuti*,' says Vincenzo. And then, turning to me – 'Welcome.'

'*Grazie*,' I say, staring at the pinks and purples and reds and yellows of the flowerbeds. There are bees and butterflies and brightly coloured birds, and a gorgeous black cat lying flat out under a tree. It makes me think of Astra; I hope she is safe.

I follow Vincenzo and Matteo into the house. If the entrance to the botanical gardens was impressive, this is something else. We walk through the bright pink flowers framing the doorway and it's as though we are enveloped in a cloud of perfume. I stop for a moment to take a deep breath – I want to remember this smell of summer and heat for ever.

The house is filled with light and air. Windows are flung open, bookcases line the walls of each room we walk past – if only we had time to look at them – and oil paintings of plants and trees fill the hallways. The floor is made of thousands of tiny, multi-coloured mosaics that form pictures of animals both mythical and real. I step carefully over scornful sphinxes and fire-breathing dragons, over leopards sprinting and eagles soaring.

Vincenzo knocks on a door and an imperious voice calls for him to come in.

The prince is sitting at his desk, writing furiously. I had expected him to be wearing a velvet suit and even – I know this is completely ridiculous – a modest crown. Instead he is dressed in a white shirt, pale blue trousers and soft leather slippers. I can feel sweat trickling down my back, but he looks as though he recently stepped out of a cool shower.

'This is Matteo D'Angelo and Nico Cloud,' says Vincenzo.

The prince stands up. He is much younger than I thought, perhaps in his early twenties.

'*Benvenuti*,' he says, as though he welcomes unexpected visitors every day.

'*Ciao*,' I say, bowing.

'Oh, you don't need to be ceremonious with me,' says the prince. 'Please, sit down.'

'I will get some drinks,' says Vincenzo.

As soon as he leaves, I panic. I fear this is a cruel trick. We too will be kidnapped and Etienne and Astra will never be rescued and Dr Hamilton won't complete her life's work. But then I remember Vincenzo knows Matteo's family. And we have till dusk to rescue Etienne and Astra. I have to believe everything is going to be OK.

285

I take a few deep breaths to calm myself down.

Matteo and I sit on adjacent chairs, opposite the open windows. The garden is much like the courtyard, packed full of plants and trees. It slopes down towards the turquoise sea and I can see a sliver of the softest white sand. I imagine vaulting out of the window, running down the slope and jumping into the most inviting sea I have ever seen.

'How was your journey from England?' asks the prince, crossing his legs and resting his hands in his lap.

'There was a huge storm,' I say, tearing my eyes away from the sea. 'It was terrifying. But we made it. Obviously.'

'I don't mean to be rude, sir . . .' says Matteo.

The prince shakes his head. 'Call me Leo, please.'

'*Grazie*, Leo,' says Matteo. 'How do you know we sailed from England?'

'A wild guess,' says Leo, smiling. 'You have clearly come a long way – you do not quite have your land legs back yet, my friend. And your friend here is English.'

'What can you tell us about the Tree of Hope?' I ask, trying not to sound rude and impatient.

Vincenzo returns with a tray. There are glasses on it, decorated with intricate floral patterns, and a jug full of chilled water with slices of lemon in it. He sets it down, pours us each a glass, then stands by the window, gazing out to sea, waiting for his next task.

'Thank you, Enzo,' says Leo, taking a glass. I finish mine in one go and, when I look up, Leo is still taking slow, careful sips.

'So,' says Leo, leaning back in his chair. '*L'albero della Speranza*. Well, I can tell you this: it really did exist.'

I jump to my feet. 'You can? How?'

Leo looks bemused. 'First, you must tell me why the Tree of Hope is so important to you.'

'We are hoping to find seeds from the tree, that have fossilised over time,' I say, sitting back down and trying to sound very serious and knowledgeable. 'We are working with a scientist . . .'

I realise I have no choice but to tell him the truth. I take another deep breath. 'A great scientist called Dr Hamilton. He who has found a way to bring fossilised seeds back to life.'

Leo looks past me at Vincenzo. Vincenzo nods at Leo as though to say, 'You can trust them.'

Leo sits upright, his blue eyes wide. Now he is interested. I keep going, my confidence building. 'Dr Hamilton thinks he could use the fossilised seeds to try and bring the Tree of Hope back to life. Then, if there is another famine or war, there will always be food. If he can bring the Tree of Hope back to life, maybe he can do the same with other trees. It could change the way we farm and it could ensure that *everyone* has access to food.'

'This is incredible news,' says Leo carefully. 'And

288

I might be able to help you. I assume you have heard of the *briccone*, the mythical bird that fed on the fruit from the Tree of Hope.'

'Yes!' I shout, excitement building. 'But it was too heavy to fly far . . .'

'Indeed. Its fossilised dung was found not far from here—'

I jump in, unable to stop myself. 'And the Tree of Hope's seeds are in the *briccone*'s dung?'

Leo nods. 'I have the seeds from that dung in a box that my mother gave me before she died.' I wait breathlessly for him continue. 'But I have a problem. I'm not sure I trust male scientists, which is strange since I am one myself. The thing is that my mother worked in secret all her life – because she was not allowed to study or work as a scientist. I do not want to hand her life's work over to a male scientist who will take all of the glory.'

I shiver. This is too good to be true! I have to imagine zipping my mouth shut so that I don't interrupt.

Aunt made me promise to protect her true identity. She didn't mention any exceptions. But we are so close to finding the fossilised seeds . . .

Leo is looking at me so intently that I fear he is reading my mind. 'I am afraid that under the circumstances I will have to decline to share the seeds with you,' he says. 'Before you leave, and while Vincenzo is cooling the horse down, will you join me in the garden? There is something I would like to show you.'

*

The afternoon heat is heavy, but every now and again a cool breeze blows up off the sea. The garden is magical, packed tightly with colourful flowers and mature trees with luminous green leaves. In the distance, the azure sea shimmers. It's impossible to think that we are here in this calm oasis, with this view, when Etienne and Astra have been kidnapped a few miles along the same coast. I try not to imagine how Astra will be suffering in this heat – or think of Etienne blaming himself for being kidnapped, as I know he will be.

Matteo and I follow Leo down the grassy path that winds through the flowers and shrubs. We stop next to a tree that looks very ordinary, even perhaps a little frail. In fact, it looks like an ancient relic.

'Let's sit here for a moment,' says Leo.

There is a bench wide enough for two people overlooking the sea, but it's in the full sun and I left the hat in the cart, so I sit underneath the shade of the ancient tree.

'This is a beautiful garden,' says Matteo, wiping beads of sweat off his brow.

'Thank you,' says Leo. He points at two nearby plants, one with white flowers and one with red. 'When I was a small boy, my *nonna* used to say that white flowers are made from tears and red flowers from blood. And I believed her!'

I run my hands through the grass, which is as green as a peacock's feathers and covered in patches of clover that are trying to take over. 'Goodness! I've found a four-leaved clover. I had one of these in my pocket when I left home, but now I've only got a handful of the tiny stones that I picked up on the beach in Cuckmere Haven. I think I must have lost the four-leaf clover somewhere.' I break its stalk and hold it up for Matteo and Leo to see.

'For good luck,' says Matteo, shading his eyes to see.

'They are also associated with dreams, you know,' says Leo.

I put the clover in the pocket of my dress, next to the stones, lie back on the cool grass and watch a wispy cloud drift across the otherwise flawless blue sky.

'My *nonna* once told me that four-leaf clover and elm are connected to prophecies. I don't really understand

292

how, but she was rarely wrong about these things. I suppose it depends if you believe stories or not.' Leo's calm voice washes over me like warm waves. I close my eyes for a moment and when I open them, the tree is covered with large red flowers. Red spheres of fruit dangle on the branches above me. As round as an apple, but slightly larger. The branches creak with their weight. I reach up and grab the ripest piece of fruit, which is split right open. The seeds are packed tightly together. They are as red as jewels and remarkably shiny, as if they have been individually polished. The seeds coat my hand in sticky red syrup, but when it starts to drip on to my dress, I let the fruit drop to the ground . . .

'Can I get you some water?' asks Leo. He is crouching over me, the back of his hand on my forehead. 'Your face is flushed – you are very hot indeed.'

'Nico! Are you OK?' says Matteo, almost elbowing the prince out of the way. 'Please get some water, Leo.'

Leo hurries back towards the house. I sit up and look at my hands. They are sticky but not red, nor are they covered with syrup. I look at the tree. Frail and dotted with tiny buds that are just forming. I look down at my dress. Red. Blood red.

'This is the Tree of Hope,' I say, feeling dizzy. 'I saw its fruit. Look! The seeds have stained my dress.'

Matteo looks at the tree. 'It is a pomegranate tree, Nico,' he says gently. 'Leo was telling us about it – he said that it's a shame we didn't visit in the autumn, when the *melograno* or pomegranate tree bears its fruit. I think you must have passed out from the heat, and Leo's words seeped into your dreams.'

'But what about the red stains on my dress?'

Matteo shrugs. 'Perhaps you were lying on those red flowers that have blown under the *melograno* tree.'

I look at the ground. It's covered in red flowers.

'But, Matteo,' I say, feeling less light-headed now.

'I didn't imagine it. I wasn't dreaming.'

'Perhaps you were dreaming. Perhaps you weren't. You will never be sure.' He smiles and pulls me to my feet.

*

Matteo puts his arm around my shoulder and I thread my arm around his waist as we walk slowly back to the house.

'Shall we tell Leo about Etienne and Astra being kidnapped?' asks Matteo. 'He might agree to give us the Tree of Hope seeds then.'

'No,' I say, more abruptly than intended. 'He will think we're going to give the seeds straight to the Kings. And I haven't thought that far ahead. We just need to persuade Leo to give us the seeds and then we can decide what to do.'

'OK, agreed,' says Matteo, dropping his voice as we approach the house.

Leo doesn't mention the pomegranate tree or my

stained dress. Instead he insists I drink two more glasses of water in his study and then he glances at the clock on the mantlepiece.

'I'm afraid I have work to do,' he says. 'Vincenzo will drop you off at the port of Palermo – he has some errands to run in town.'

He pauses, as though half hoping that I will say something important. *This is my final chance to persuade him*, I think.

I clear my throat. 'I ran away from home. I didn't know it at the time, but there was a reason: to end up here, in this room with you. I persuaded everyone on *Anthos* – Dr Hamilton's ship – to sail to Sicily to find the fossilised seeds from the Tree of Hope. I believed the tree existed when no one else did. I believe in science but I believe in myths too. Myths that a grandmother tells her grandchild. Stories that are passed down through generations. Maybe they change slightly each time they are retold – but they are still more or less true. I know you believe in the power of science and myths too!'

Leo sits and thinks. He glances at the clock. He thinks some more.

Matteo bites his nails.

I bite my lower lip.

'Leo,' I say quietly. 'Dr Hamilton is convinced he can recreate the Tree of Hope. But he will never know if you don't let us take the fossilised seeds. And who else is going to be able to try and bring the Tree back to life? I know you worry about bad and greedy men – but I am helping Dr Hamilton and I'm not a bad man. Or even a man.' I pause. I'll try one last thing and then we will have to leave. 'Seeds mean everything to me. They are going to be my life's work. Even if I have to work in a shed outside the science department of a university.'

'You sound very much like my mother,' he says thoughtfully. 'You saw the magic in the tree just now . . .'

I gasp. So it was the Tree of Hope!

'. . . You know, I think, that science can be magical.' He stands up. He takes a key out of his pocket and uses it to open a desk hidden behind a huge green potted plant, much like those in the hot house at the botanical garden. He removes a plain box tied up with a red ribbon and stands in the middle of his study, holding the box in both hands.

I stand up and walk towards him.

I put my hands out. 'If you give me the Tree of Hope's fossilised seeds, I promise to take care of them. I promise to let you know if Dr Hamilton succeeds. I promise that your mother will be remembered.'

Now that I am so close to the seeds, I can't bear to think of handing them over to Otis King. I can't bear to think of him then passing them on to greedy scientists interested only in money. We have to find another way of rescuing Etienne and Astra!

Leo shuts his eyes and gives me the box, which I place carefully at the bottom of my puffin bag. I want to pinch myself and see if I am dreaming. The clock chimes four. Dusk is approaching.

20

'*Grazie mille*, Enzo!' shouts Matteo, as we jump off the cart. '*A dopo!* See you soon.'

'Thank you, Vincenzo,' I say, grabbing Matteo by the hand and pulling him through the crowds of people who are wandering up and down the edge of the port in the finest clothes I have ever seen.

'Slow down,' urges Matteo. 'Let's not run so quickly we fall into the sea.'

I let go of his hand and hold on to my puffin bag with both hands, just in case. Imagine if the seeds fell into the sea now, or if someone stole my bag and, having no idea of their value, threw the seeds away!

We pound along the long wooden walkway, alongside the fishing boats, making a ridiculous racket. I trip over a loose board and my puffin bag flies out of my hands and lands on the edge of the walkway. A gust of wind and it will fall into the sea.

'Matteo!' I shout.

He is on his knees, grabbing the handles of the bag.

'*Grazie mille*,' I say breathlessly, clutching the bag to my chest. I check my pocket for the tiny stones and the four-leaf clover. No more time to waste. We need to get to the fort and face the Kings.

We run run run.

The rowing boat is tied up to the side of *Anthos*, the telescope placed under the front seat. We just need to get in the boat and **row row row**.

*

Matteo insists on rowing while I sit at the front, looking anxiously through the telescope. My bag is beneath my seat, so that it doesn't get splashed.

'I can't see anyone out by the fort,' I say, adjusting the telescope. 'Do you think this is a trick?'

'It could be,' says Matteo. 'But I doubt it. We have what they want and vice versa.'

'I can't see any boats at all out there. Hang on, I think there's a ship moored in the shadows, right by the rocks.'

I shiver. The air seems to be changing and taking on a chill.

'Sea fret,' says Matteo, huffing and puffing as he pulls on the oars. 'We need to stop rowing and wait for it to pass.'

The wet mist swirls around us and encloses us in a cloud of thick, sticky dampness. Matteo rests the oars and we drift for a few minutes, waiting for the sea fret to dissolve. I think of Astra, not much more than a kitten, lying on my chest, her tiny body vibrating – and of course Etienne, who will be wondering if we are ever going to come and save him.

'What are we going to do, Matteo?' I ask, turning to look at him.

'We have to be patient,' he says, doing his best to offer a reassuring smile.

'We should carry on,' I say. 'Slowly.'

'But I can't see a thing!'

'Just do it,' I say. 'Please.'

He dips the oars back in the water and we edge slowly forwards. It's as though we are in a dream, rowing endlessly forward into nothingness. We can't see or hear anything, only taste the salt hanging in the air. The sun could have set and we wouldn't have a clue.

I keep the telescope glued to my eye. Without warning, the ship moored by the rocks looms out of the greyness. It is still and silent, but it appears to be sneering at us, flexing its muscles, telling us it is much bigger, stronger and more important than us.

'Matteo!' I gasp. 'Pull the oars in again. Right now!'

He does so immediately. We drift towards the ship.

The sea fret swirls in circles as though it's dancing. Just for a moment, it clears. 'I can't see anyone on the deck,' I say.

Behind me, a loud whack, a crack and a splash.

I turn quickly and the telescope drops out of my hands.

Matteo is nowhere to be seen.

'Nico!'

He is in the water, gasping and flailing. Someone must have snuck up behind us in a rowing boat and hit him on the head.

'I can't swim!'

How is that even possible? A life spent at sea and he has never learned to swim . . .

I look around wildly, trying to see the assailant.

I can't see a thing in the thick grey air, but I can just about make out the distant sound of oars pushing through the water.

'Here,' I say, kneeling down in the middle of the boat and leaning over as far as I dare. 'Grab my hand.'

I don't know if I'm strong enough.

He grasps my hand, but the water is slippery and I lose him.

'Nico,' he splutters.

'Again,' I shout. 'We can do this. Hold tight!'

He takes my hand again, palm to palm, and I hold on as firmly as I can. The blisters from holding on so firmly to the wheel in the storm had faded but now they feel red raw again.

I hold his hand with both of mine. I **pull pull pull**, closing my eyes, holding my breath. *I am strong. Stronger than I think. I* can *do this.*

'For Etienne,' I say, panting. 'Do this for him.'

Matteo tries to grab the boat with his right hand again.

'*Per aspera ad astra*,' I say. 'Come on, Matteo. I know you can do it.'

His right hand grips tightly on to the side of the boat. His face is full of determination. I let go of his left hand and he holds on to the boat with both hands, takes a deep breath and yanks himself up and over the side. His clothes hang from him, soaked and heavy.

'Matteo!' I throw my arms around him. He smells of fear and sea and something metallic, like iron. Blood. I gently touch the gash on his head and he flinches.

'Otis,' he growls, sitting down, grabbing the oars and heading straight for the ship.

*

The sea fret has lifted. We are so close to the ship that we can see the ladder dangled over the side. For us, I assume. Otis's rowing boat is already tied to a metal loop on the side of the ship, the oars dropped hastily in the middle.

We tie our own rowing boat to the lowest rung of the ladder and climb it quickly, before we have time to think of the consequences.

'What if this is the wrong ship?' I whisper to Matteo as we clamber on to the deck. Then I stop. 'Can you hear that?' I ask. A muted *miaow*, like the cat version of a whisper.

I see Etienne first. A handkerchief has been secured around his mouth and he is tied to the mast with an old rope that has been wound around his waist and ankles, making him look as though he's in a children's book about pirates. He is clutching something to his chest, firmly but with great tenderness. *Astra.*

'Astra!' I say. 'Etienne!'

'Stop!' Otis appears from nowhere, as usual, and stands on the deck in front of Etienne and Astra. He isn't holding a sword or a knife; he doesn't need to. He has what we want.

'Hello again, Otis. Where's your father?' I ask, hoping my voice doesn't sound as shaky to Otis as it does in my head.

He ignores me and looks at Matteo. 'That's a nasty gash, someone very strong must have whacked you pretty hard. I didn't think your girlfriend here would be strong enough to save you. And now she's got your blood all over her dress . . .'

You know nothing, Otis King. His mocking tone reminds me of my twin brothers. I force myself to take no notice. Just words. Empty, hollow, irrelevant words.

Etienne is trying to say something, but his voice

is muffled.

'What's that, Etienne?' asks Otis, smirking. 'Sorry, can't hear you.'

Matteo stands very still, the seawater dripping from his clothes. He is just about managing to keep a lid on his anger, but if he is provoked again, I know he will erupt like a volcano. Instead he smiles at Etienne and mouths the words, 'don't worry'.

'Otis,' I say sternly. 'Where is your father?'

'None of your business,' he says, shaking his curly head. He offers an upturned palm. 'Hand over the fossilised seeds.'

Tempting though it is to kick him in the shins, I do my best to ignore his rudeness. Instead I open my bag, carefully place the prince's box on the deck and take a step back. Otis kneels down and flips the lid open. There, inside, lying on a piece of green silk, are a dozen seed-shaped stones.

'This is it?' he asks, narrowing his eyes at me. 'These are the real thing?'

'What did you expect? They are millions of years old. They aren't going to be blood red like the fruit that bore them. Do you not understand anything about paleobotany?'

I can feel Matteo pulling a 'stop it' face at me, but I don't care. Otis has to believe me and this is the only way.

'If you don't want them,' I continue, looking Otis straight in the eyes, 'we will find another way to rescue Etienne and Astra.'

'Ha!' says Otis. 'We have a proper crew, you know. They will be back from Palermo any moment. You will see. You have no choice but to do as we say.'

'Free Etienne,' I say. 'Free my cat.'

'Does friendship really mean that much to you?' asks Otis. 'You would hand over the most valuable seeds in the world for the sake of the boy and the cat?'

I nod. It's true. I didn't know it was true till now, but it is. I might be imagining it, but for a split second I'm pretty sure Otis looks sad – after all, he is a boy with no friends and a mean father. I realise that I could have been that child, had I stayed at home.

'Free Etienne,' I say, more confidently this time.

'No,' says Otis casually. 'Father says we will have to wait until the seeds have germinated.'

But they don't even understand the science! Aunt Ruth isn't even sure she can germinate the fossilised seeds. Best not to alert them to this.

'Then we shall have to wait around for months until the seedlings grow into saplings,' I say. 'Only when it's a young tree will you know if it is indeed the Tree of Hope.'

'I don't believe you found these in the botanical garden,' says Otis eventually. 'I think you are a liar.'

Matteo steps forwards towards Otis. I put my arm in front of him.

'You are right,' I say. 'We did not find them in the botanical garden. Matteo and I were given these seeds by a prince.'

Just then, a door slams at the other end of the ship and there, in a bright red velvet cloak, his black curly hair not quite as wild as his son's, is Herman. He strides across the deck, his heavy black boots making a dull thud as he goes. He stops in front of me.

'So,' he says, narrowing his black eyes. 'You are the famous Nico Cloud.'

I nod.

He puts his hand inside the depths of his cloak and triumphantly pulls out my leather notebook.

'I'm surprised you needed to kidnap anyone, if you had my notebook,' I said. 'It would have led you where you needed to go.'

Herman glares at his son. 'Perhaps if Otis hadn't dropped your notebook in the sea and the drawings hadn't all become smudged we wouldn't be standing here now – we'd be sailing back to London to pick up our huge reward for the Tree of Hope's seeds instead of resorting to a kidnapping . . .'

Otis looks at the deck.

'You should be kinder to your son,' I say.

'And you shouldn't be so careless,' sneers Herman. 'It obviously runs in the family.'

'I have no idea what . . .' I say, my voice faltering.

He tosses my notebook into the sea.

'Please thank your aunt for doing all the hard work in her little cabin on *Anthos*,' he says. 'She should have been more careful when disguising herself as a man.'

'Your *aunt*?' gasps Matteo. 'Dr Hamilton is your . . . aunt?'

I ignore him; I can't take my eyes off Herman. He turns to his son, snatches the box from his hands and stares at the seeds inside.

At that moment, Astra yowls. I turn. She jumps out of Etienne's arms and her little body skids across the deck. I follow her, but I'm too late. She has skidded straight through the gap where the ladder dangles down to our rowing boat.

'Astra! Astra!' I shout desperately, leaning over the side of the ship. I can't see a thing in the dense fog but I can hear her scrabbling in the water.

Then there's a loud splash and an arm appears in the sea and scoops Astra up. It all happens so quickly that I barely have time to register what is going on. A figure climbs up the ladder carrying Astra – I expect to see Matteo, but it's Otis. It's the pirate boy who walks across the deck, his shirt and trousers dripping with seawater, and hands me my sodden cat.

'Why on earth did you do that, Otis?' asks Herman, staring at his son. 'It's only an animal for goodness' sake. We have more important things to do!'

'Thank you,' I say, taking Astra from Otis's outstretched hands, and wrapping her shivering body inside my bag. 'That was brave.'

Otis shrugs. Then he sees his father staring at him and seems to remember that he is meant to be mean, not kind. He takes a knife out of his pocket and holds the blade close to the skin on Etienne's neck.

'You can leave now,' says Otis, looking at me and Etienne. 'You have the cat. We will keep your friend until we find out whether these seeds are the right ones.'

Etienne's eyes widen. He gulps and the knife draws a pin prick of blood on his neck.

Neither myself nor Matteo has a knife. Or, in fact, a weapon of any sort. I thought the seeds were enough. I thought the seeds were everything.

The early evening sun pushes through the sea fret. I can hear voices in the distance. At first, I assume they must be coming from the fort, but slowly I realise they are in the water nearby.

The voices subside and in their place is an unmistakable creak and rattle of an approaching ship. I turn to face it. Its wooden figurehead looms out of the greyness, almost as though it's not attached to a ship at all. The woman with a bleeding neck is triumphantly holding a sword aloft. That is why her dress was red in my dream: the sword. Or, perhaps, like me, she is stained with the juices of the Tree of Life fruit. I blink hard. *Is she smiling?* The ship sails past and I see that its deck is packed not with ghostly figures, but with sacks of wheat.

Santa Lucia.

When I turn my attention back to the deck, everyone is looking at me. Perhaps I was dreaming again. Perhaps I was the only one who saw Santa Lucia on the ghost ship. Perhaps she only made herself visible to me. I suddenly remember the captain's story: Santa Lucia gave her riches to the poor. She didn't wait to hear their stories, she didn't judge them for having nothing to eat, she just wanted to help. She was right – we can't always understand what others have been through.

I take a determined step towards Otis. 'Are the scientists in London making you do this?'

His blue eyes are suddenly wild as the first time I met him. He nods and starts to say something, but his father clamps his hand over his son's mouth and he drops the knife. Quick as a flash, I pick it up and cut the cloth covering Etienne's mouth.

'Stop!' shouts Otis, grabbing my wrist and wrenching the knife away.

Etienne sucks a mouthful of air into his lungs and then sighs it all back out again. 'I'm not a boy of many words, but I will say this, Otis King. I've been thinking about it while I've been tied up and gagged. When I was very young, my mother was washed overboard during a violent storm. I could have spent my life being angry at the world. But I found the courage to be kind. I have a father who loves me and a great friend.' He looks at me. 'Two great friends.'

Otis swallows hard. He steps away from his father.

'Putting a knife at my throat isn't the kind of courage I admire,' says Etienne. 'Being kind can be hard, but I think you have kindness in you, Otis. Of that I am certain.'

Otis walks over to Etienne, cuts the rope and rips it away from Etienne's body.

He stands opposite Herman, his head held high. 'You are right. We had no choice. Father fell into debt and the scientists offered to pay it off.'

'Did you have no other way of earning money?' I ask.

Herman says nothing.

'No,' says Otis quietly. 'Father tried everything. We even lost our home. We didn't know when our next meal might be . . .'

'I'm sorry to hear that,' says Matteo. 'Living hand to mouth is tough.'

Otis takes the box of fossilised seeds out of his father's hands and gives it back to me. 'You should keep the seeds,' he says. 'They belong to you, not to some scientists in London that we have never even met.'

'But, Otis . . .' protests Herman.

'We will find another way to pay back our debt, Father,' says Otis.

Herman gives an exasperated sigh, then turns, cloak billowing out behind him, and storms off down the deck.

I put Astra down, pick up the box and place it carefully at the bottom of my bag, even though the seeds I gave Otis are really just the seed-shaped pebbles I picked up on the beach at Cuckmere Haven. The real Tree of Hope seeds – which look as though they are lit from within – are in my pocket, next to the four-leaf clover.

I kiss Astra's nose and place her on top of the box; she is still shivering, but her coat is all fluffed up again.

'Thank you, Otis,' I say.

Otis nods. 'Father and I were accidental pirates, weren't we? You should go, quickly, before the crew get here. Father might change his mind about letting you go.'

'Otis,' I say. 'You could come with us. There is plenty of room aboard *Anthos*.'

Matteo and Etienne look confused for a moment – I know it's the kind of thing we should discuss first, but there isn't time – and then they both nod. Not exactly enthusiastically, but I knew they wouldn't turn him away.

'Thank you,' says Otis. 'But my place is here, with Father. I have sometimes thought about running away – I almost asked you to take me with you on the beach at Cuckmere Haven, but I couldn't leave Father on his own. He isn't always mean – I think he is just ashamed that we have had to behave badly to try and pay back our debts.'

I think about that day on the beach, when he stole my notebook. He looked so mean. I had no idea he too wanted to run away . . .

'Are you sure?' I ask. He nods vigorously and I believe him. He looks lighter somehow, I think. As though he's relieved to have talked about it.

I put my hand on Otis's arm. I'm not going to tell him that I didn't give him the real seeds. There's no point in humiliating him further. 'My aunt – Dr Hamilton, I mean – will be so grateful you changed your mind about the seeds. This is our chance to make the world a better place and you have helped with that – if only by persuading us to sail to Sicily so that we got our hands on the seeds first! In exchange, I am going to tell Dr Hamilton of your kindness and see if she can help your father by finding him some honest work or by raising funds some other way. No one should have to worry about where their next meal is coming from. Write to Dr Hamilton and she will write back to you. I promise.'

'After everything we've done?' asks Otis, his voice so soft it's almost inaudible.

'Yes,' I say. And I mean it. 'I am sure Dr Hamilton will understand too.'

'Until we meet again,' says Matteo to Otis, but he has gone.

Etienne is already halfway down the ladder, and we follow him quickly, in case Herman reappears.

'Poor Otis,' I say, holding on to Astra tightly as I clamber on to my seat at the back of the rowing boat.

'I think he will be fine,' says Matteo, untying the rope and coiling it up neatly in our rowing boat. 'If his father doesn't have to worry about money, he might be more warm-hearted to Otis.'

'I hope so,' I say, looking at the Kings' ship as we push away from it.

We sit in silence for a moment.

Etienne coughs and I crash back to the present, into the rowing boat, with my kitten on my knee.

'Were you really willing to swap the Tree of Hope seeds to save Astra and me?' asks Etienne.

'It's a long story! Yes and no.' I can't see his face, but Etienne's shoulders drop. I shouldn't really tease him after his ordeal. 'But mostly yes.'

'Wow,' says Etienne and I know he is smiling as he plunges the oars into the sea.

*

The mist dances in front of our boat, higher and higher into the air, until it vanishes as quickly as it appeared. The sky is a brilliant orange, with streaks of pink and wisp of dark clouds. The boys don't mention Saint Lucia's ship so neither do I. I don't care if I was the only one to see her. It doesn't matter. She gave me courage when I needed it most. But I have a feeling Etienne saw it too, because of all the things he said about kindness.

We sit in comfortable silence for a while, listening to the oars push methodically through the water. I am waiting for Matteo's barrage of questions and finally he turns and looks at me with an amused expression.

'So,' he says, slowly and deliberately. 'Dr Hamilton is your aunt.'

I nod slowly. My aunt. I am incredibly proud to be her niece, but, for the first time I realise I love her like she is my mother.

Matteo goes on. 'We knew she was a woman, but . . .'

'You *all* knew?' I ask, my mouth dropping open.

'Papà guessed Dr Hamilton's secret on the trip to Siberia. He told me shortly before we arrived in Palermo, in case the Kings tried to use it against us. Anyway, it's no big deal. She had work to do and it was our job to let her get on with it.'

'She's some aunt,' says Etienne, hauling the oars through the water.

Matteo twists his body around so he's completely facing me. 'How did you manage not to tell me and Etienne? I didn't think you would be any good at keeping secrets.'

'That's not fair . . .' I realise that he is teasing me and I burst out laughing. 'It *has* been hard.'

My body relaxes. I hadn't realised how tense I was. No more secrets. Not from these new brothers of mine. I take Astra out of the puffin bag – which has seen almost as many adventures as me – and place her on my knee. She stands on her back legs, places her front paws on my chest and buffs my face. She pushes her head hard against my forehead, as though thanking me for rescuing her not once, but twice.

Etienne rows, smoothly and quickly, back towards the port of Palermo. I put my hand in the pocket of my dress and check again for the Tree of Hope seeds. I can almost feel them glow in the palm of my hand as though they are ready to be brought back to life. When *Anthos* looms into view, I see Aunt Ruth on the deck with her pipe in her mouth and her telescope glued to her eye. She is willing us home.

The Times

July 30 1833

THE UNIQUE TREE BRINGING HOPE TO THE WORLD

Dr Ruth Hamilton and her adopted daughter, Nico Cloud Hamilton,
standing next to the reanimated Tree of Hope.

Yesterday Dr Ruth Hamilton was elected the first female member of the Institute of International Paleobotanists (IIP) for her ground-breaking research into the regeneration of fossilised seeds. Her work in bringing the Tree of Hope back to life has changed scientists' perception of the importance of fossilised seeds. It is now widely accepted that seeds are of vital importance for the future of mankind.

Dr Hamilton is currently raising funds for a Seed Vault, in which millions of seeds can be safely stored for future use.

'I am hoping that farmers will send us samples of seeds from around the world,' said Dr Hamilton. 'Many people have experienced famine and war and we know that advances in technology will eventually change agricultural practices – and not necessarily for the best.'

Last month, Dr Hamilton, who conducted most of her research aboard a ship called *Anthos*, took great delight in helping to demolish the 'dusty old shed' in which she had previously been forced to work while carrying out research at her former university. 'It was truly a pleasure to get rid of that old thing,' she said yesterday. 'It's high time women were on equal footing with men when it comes to science. We are not nearly there yet, but having my own office at my new university and being accepted into the IIP is a fantastic start.'

Dr Hamilton was assisted in her research by her adopted daughter, Nico Cloud Hamilton, who also has a great passion for fossils and seeds. Both made it clear that they could not have completed their research without invaluable help from Prince Leonardo Esposito of Sicily, his late mother Francesca and their crew aboard *Anthos*, including Matteo D'Angelo and Etienne Levi.

They confirmed that Otis and Herman King are not in fact pirates as some newspapers have recently claimed, but two desperate people who had been offered a large sum of money by an unnamed group of scientists in London to steal Dr Hamilton's research. The aforementioned scientists are currently under investigation while the Kings' debt has been paid off by Dr Hamilton, who sold one of her much sought-after illustrations of fossilised seeds to do so.

While trying to ensure her calico cat, Astra, didn't escape the confines of a bag embroidered with an odd-looking puffin, Cloud Hamilton also managed to share her clear message for the world with us. 'Fossils are the past, but seeds are the future.'

Acknowledgements

Writing this book was a pretty solitary affair, since we were deep into lockdown. However, there are, as always, a series of people without whom The Ship of Cloud and Stars *wouldn't exist. I owe all these people a thank you and a bag of warm Sicilian* arancini . . .

Bonnie, for navigating the pandemic with me and persuading me that this book had to be finished.

Mum, for everything.

Andrea Cangioli for using his Sicilian heritage to scrutinize the European leg of the story.

Riccardo Berna and his Tuscan albero di melograno.

Adrian Gallop for some really sound advice.

David Attenborough, who got me thinking about fossils and seeds in the first place.

A massive debt of gratitude to my editor, Polly Lyall-Grant. It was a pleasure to share my ideas for Nico's European adventure, even during a global lockdown. Especially during a global lockdown – thank goodness I could escape to Sicily in my head. Thank you also to Maeve LG for providing the visual inspiration for Astra. Cats rule.

George Ermos, for bringing Nico, Matteo and Co. to life with your gorgeous illustrations.

Everyone at Hachette Children's Group for their tireless enthusiam: Martina Borg, Alice Duggan, Ruth Girmatsion, Annabel El-Kerim, Genevieve Herr, Felicity Highet, Jen Hudson and Dom Kingston.

The Society of Authors for the grant that facilitated the writing of this book. Since grants have been massively oversubscribed in the past few years, I am particularly grateful.

If you would like to read more about female scientists being remembered for their cooking and not their innovations, check out Women in Science: 50 Fearless Pioneers who Changed

the World, *written and illustrated by Rachel Ignotofsky* or Headstrong: 52 Women Who Changed Science – and the World *by Rachel Swaby.*

Finally, a few explanations about names in the book. Astra's is in homage to Dame Sarah Gilbert and Catherine Green, who delivered the AstraZeneca vaccine in record time. This is a more nebulous reference, but nonetheless an important one: Dr Ruth Hamilton takes her name from the late Ruth Bader Ginsburg, who made it her life's work to fight tirelessly for a woman's right to be heard, especially when she was associate justice of the Supreme Court of the United States between 1993 and 2020. Rest in power, RBG.

P.S. the Tree of Hope didn't really exist . . . did it?

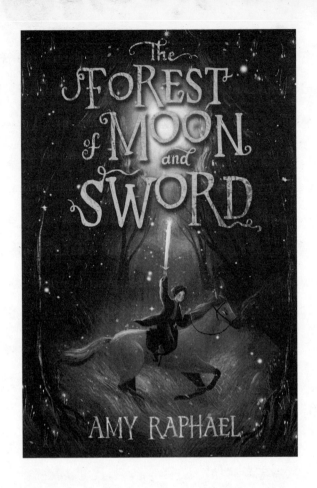

Read Amy Raphael's beautiful debut children's novel.

When Art's mother is accused of witchcraft and captured, she is determined to get her back – at any cost. But will she spot the signs from the omens? Will she reach her mother, before it's too late?

A lyrical adventure with folklore at its heart . . .

Praise for *The Forest of Moon and Sword*

"A sumptuously imagined children's debut"

Telegraph

"A fast paced, single minded adventure.

Female bravery is a given"

Observer

"A wonderful book"

Piers Torday

'Art's journey into the wicked heart of the witch

trials is immersive, and vividly drawn'

Hannah Tooke, author of *The Unadoptables*